W9-CEW-383

Benny
on the Beach

by ED and Diego Arandojo

PICTURE WINDOW BOOKS
a capstone imprint

First published in the United States in 2020
by Picture Window Books, an imprint of Capstone
1710 Roe Crest Drive
North Mankato, Minnesota 56003
www.capstonepub.com

First published in Spain in 2009 by Bang Ediciones.
SL Casanova, 75, 1-1, 08011 Barcelona
Illustrations copyright © 2009 by Bang Ediciones.
English text copyright © 2020 by Capstone.

Library of Congress Cataloging-in-Publication Data
is available on the Library of Congress website.
ISBN: 978-1-5158-6136-2 (library binding)
ISBN: 978-1-5158-6142-3 (eBook PDF)

Summary: At first, Benny isn't too excited about
spending a day on the beach. But then the young boy
digs up a living, breathing woolly mammoth, and a day
of adventure begins.

Editorial Credits
Maxi Luchini and Ed, collection directors; Immaculada Bordell,
collection designer

Printed and bound in the USA.
PA100

How to Read a Wordless Graphic Novel

Wordless graphic novels are easy to read. Boxes called panels show you how to follow the story. Look at the panels from left to right and top to bottom.

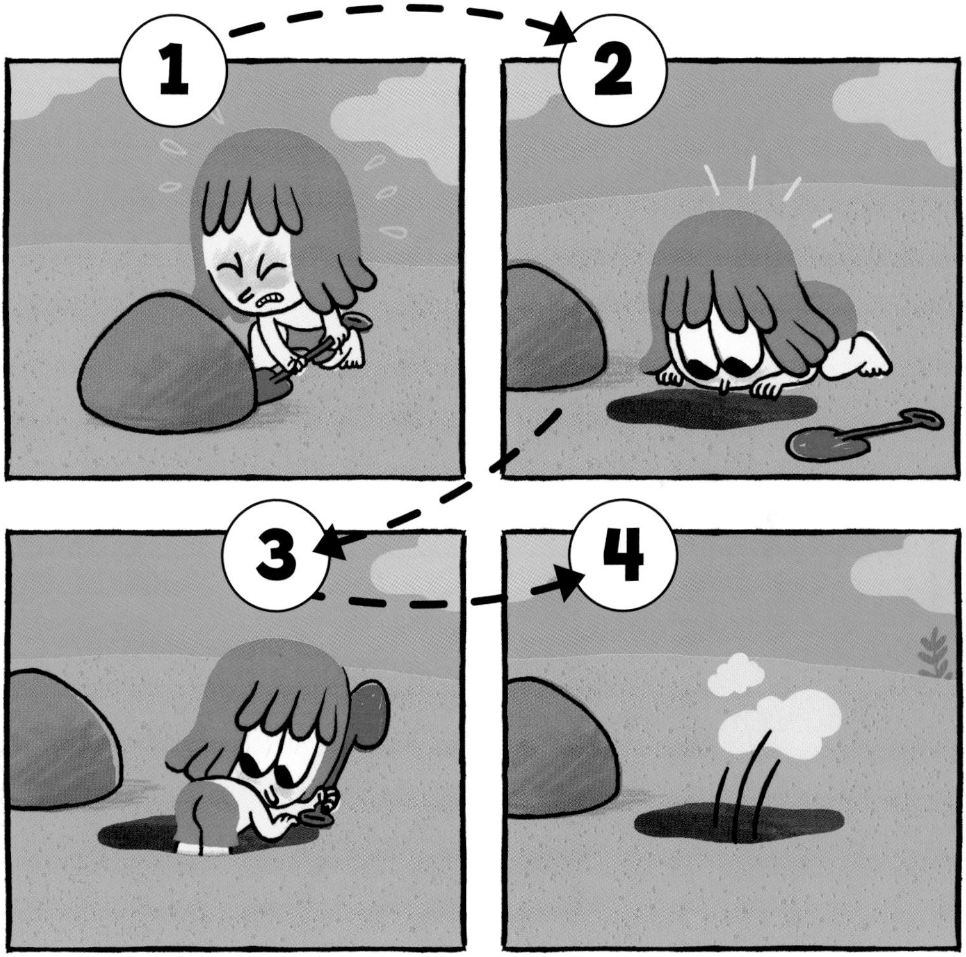
1
2
3
4

The pictures work together to tell the whole story!

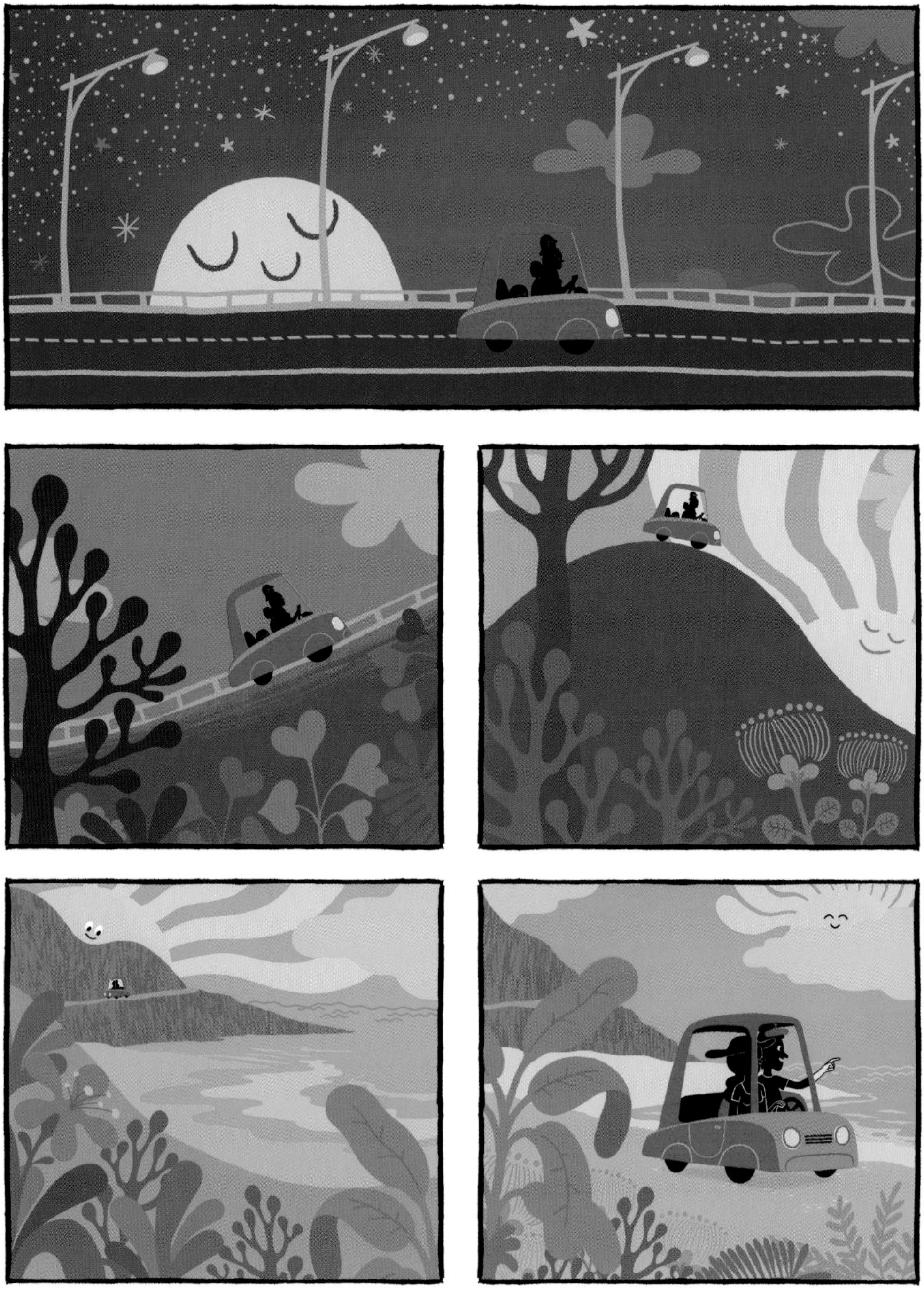

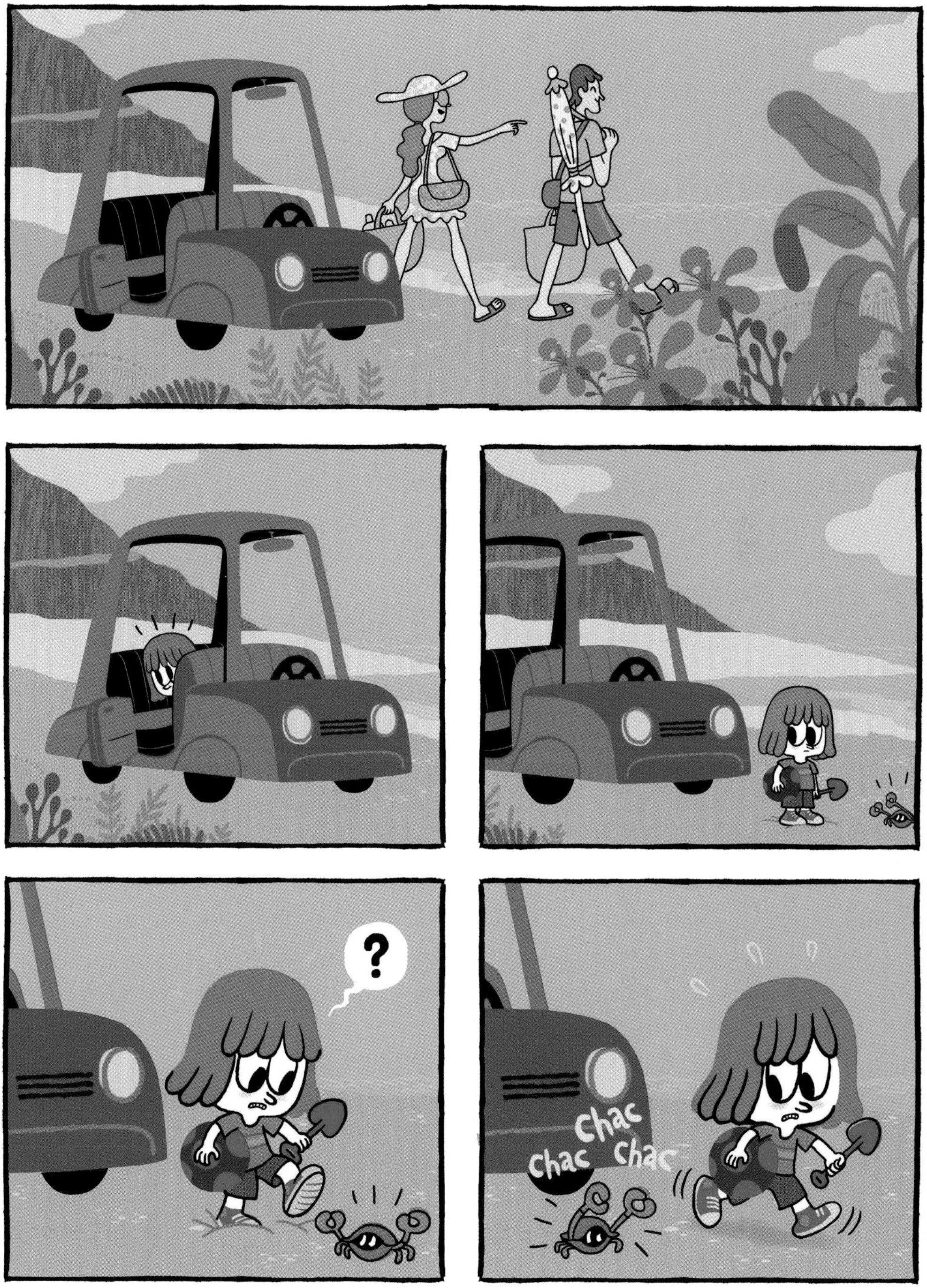
?
Chac
Chac
Chac

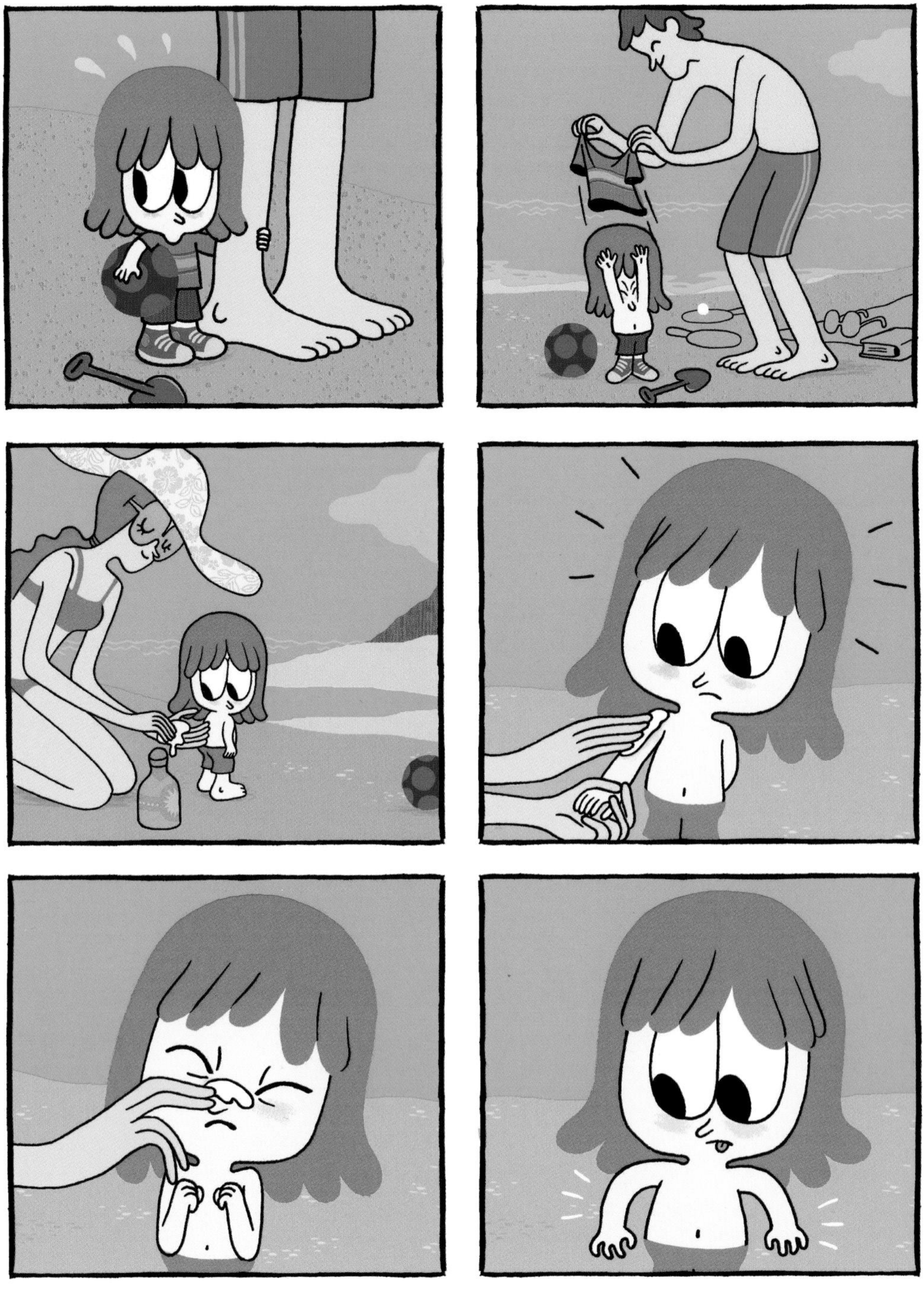

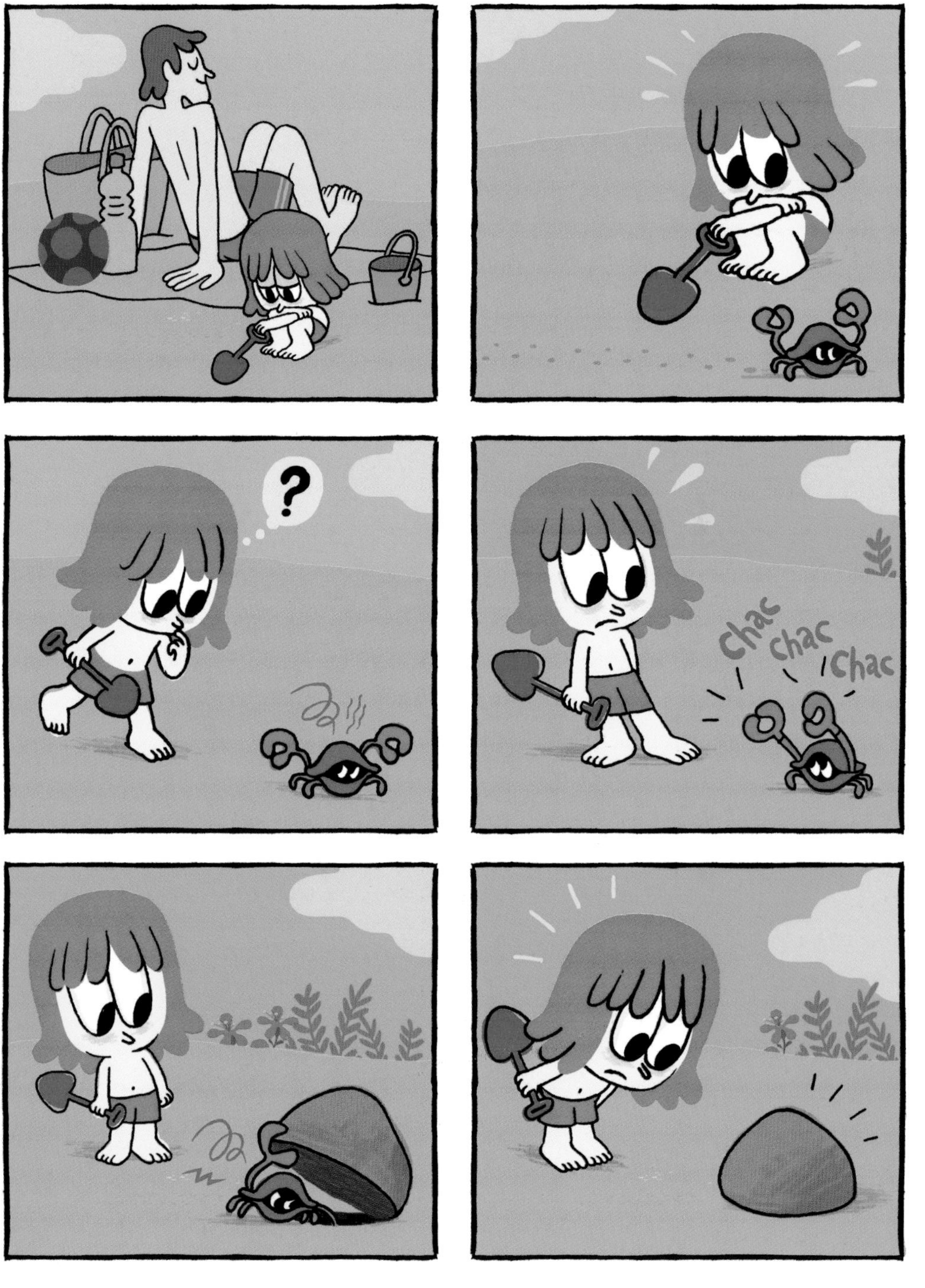
?
Chac
chac
Chac

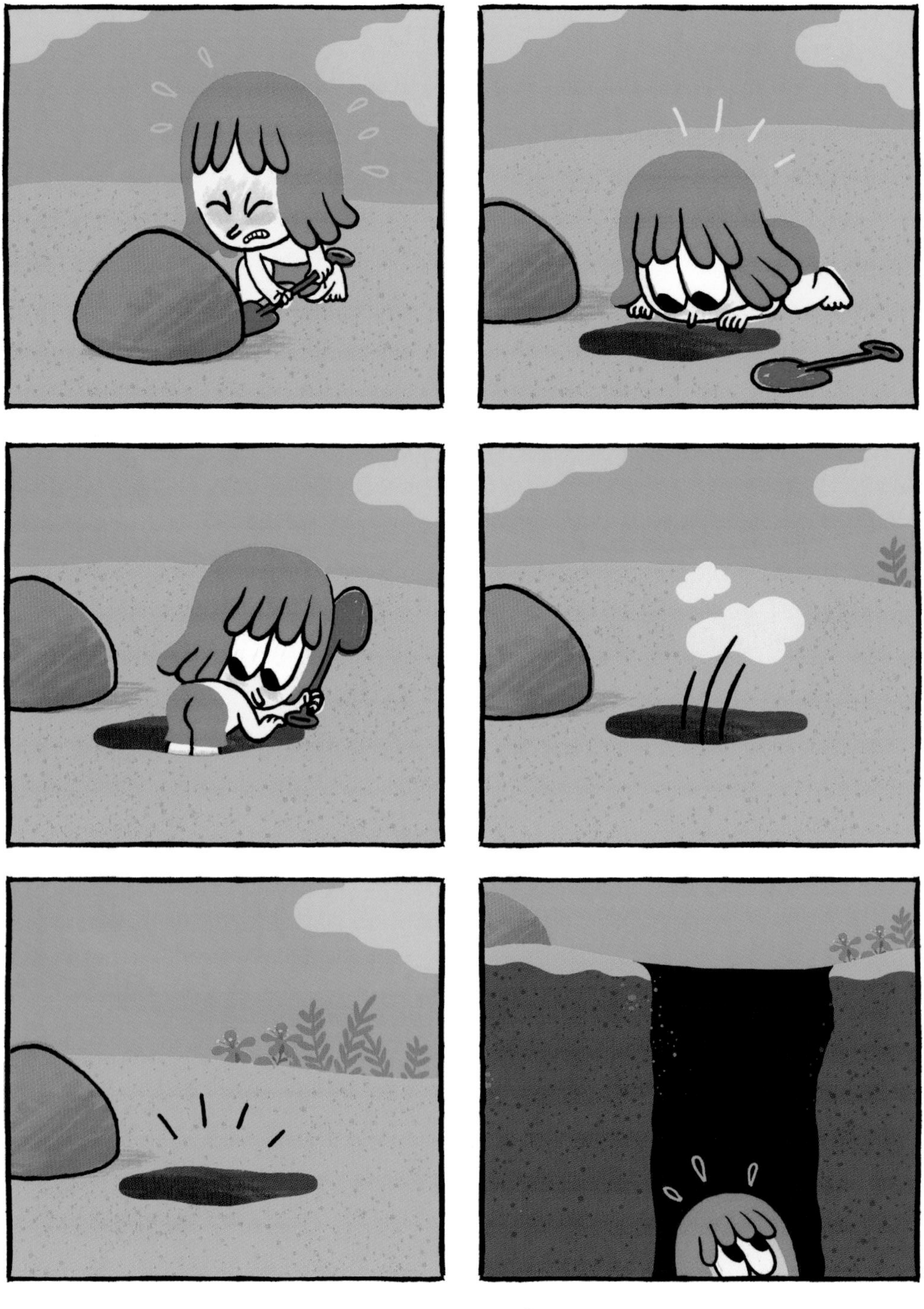

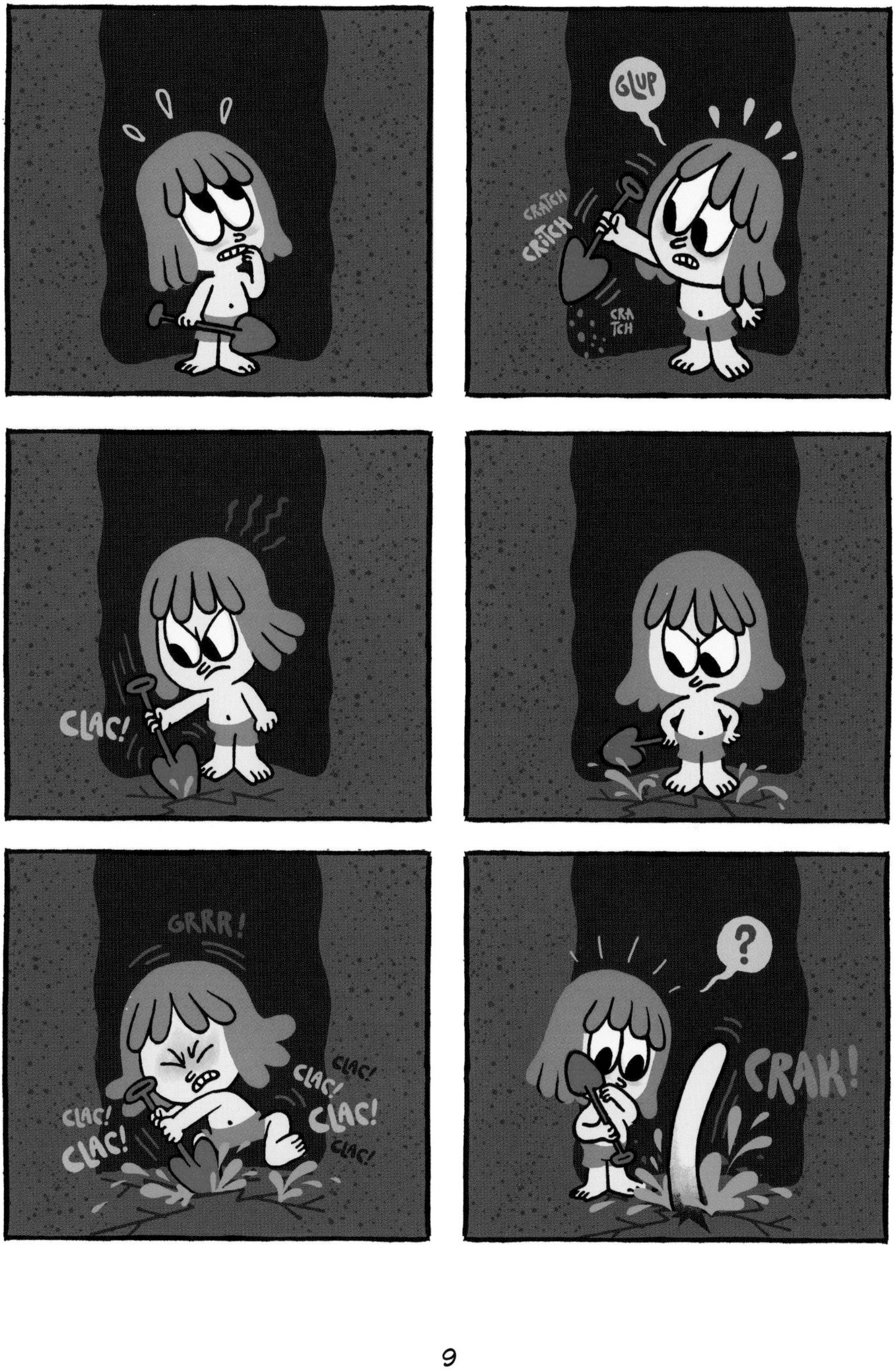
GLUP
CRATCH
CRITCH
CRA
TCH
CLAC!
GRRR!
CLAC!
CLAC!
CLAC!
CLAC!
CLAC!
CLAC!
?
CRAK!

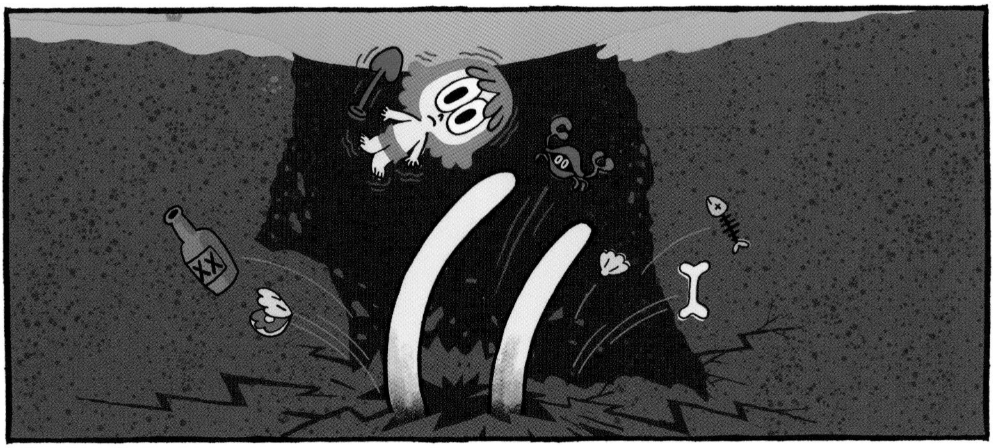

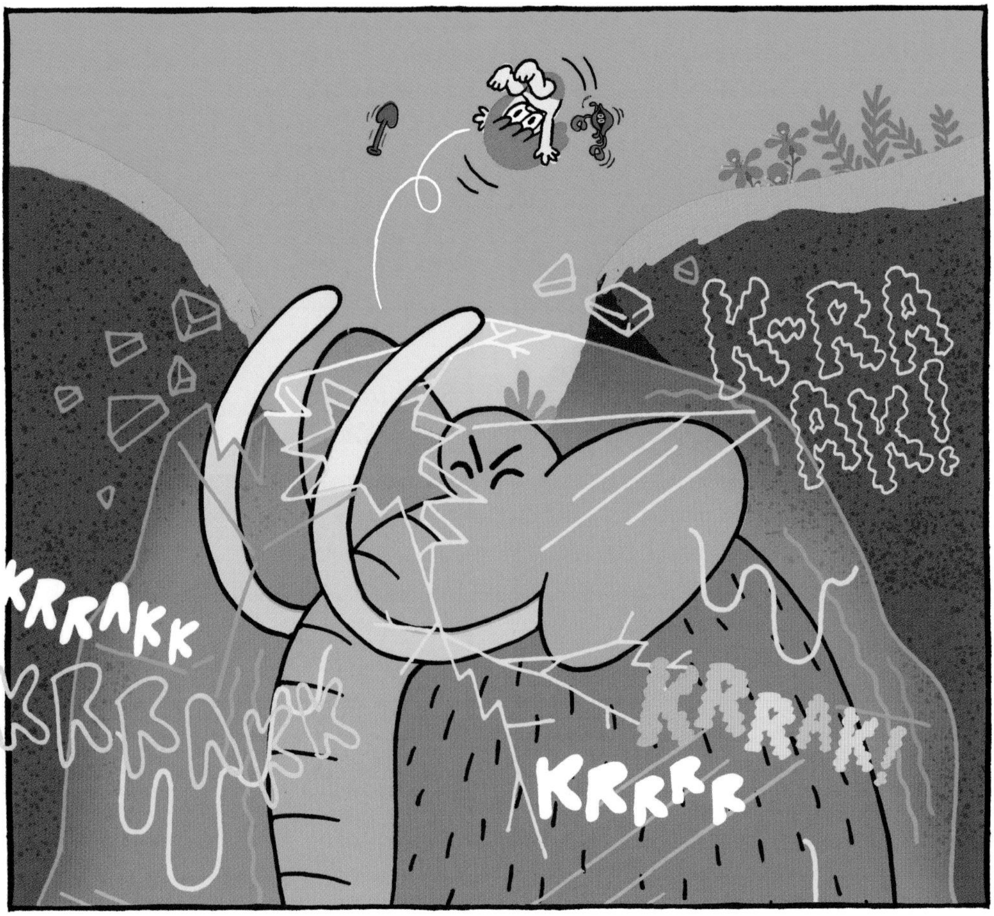
K-RRA
AM!
KRRAKK
KRRAKK
KRRAK!
KRRRR

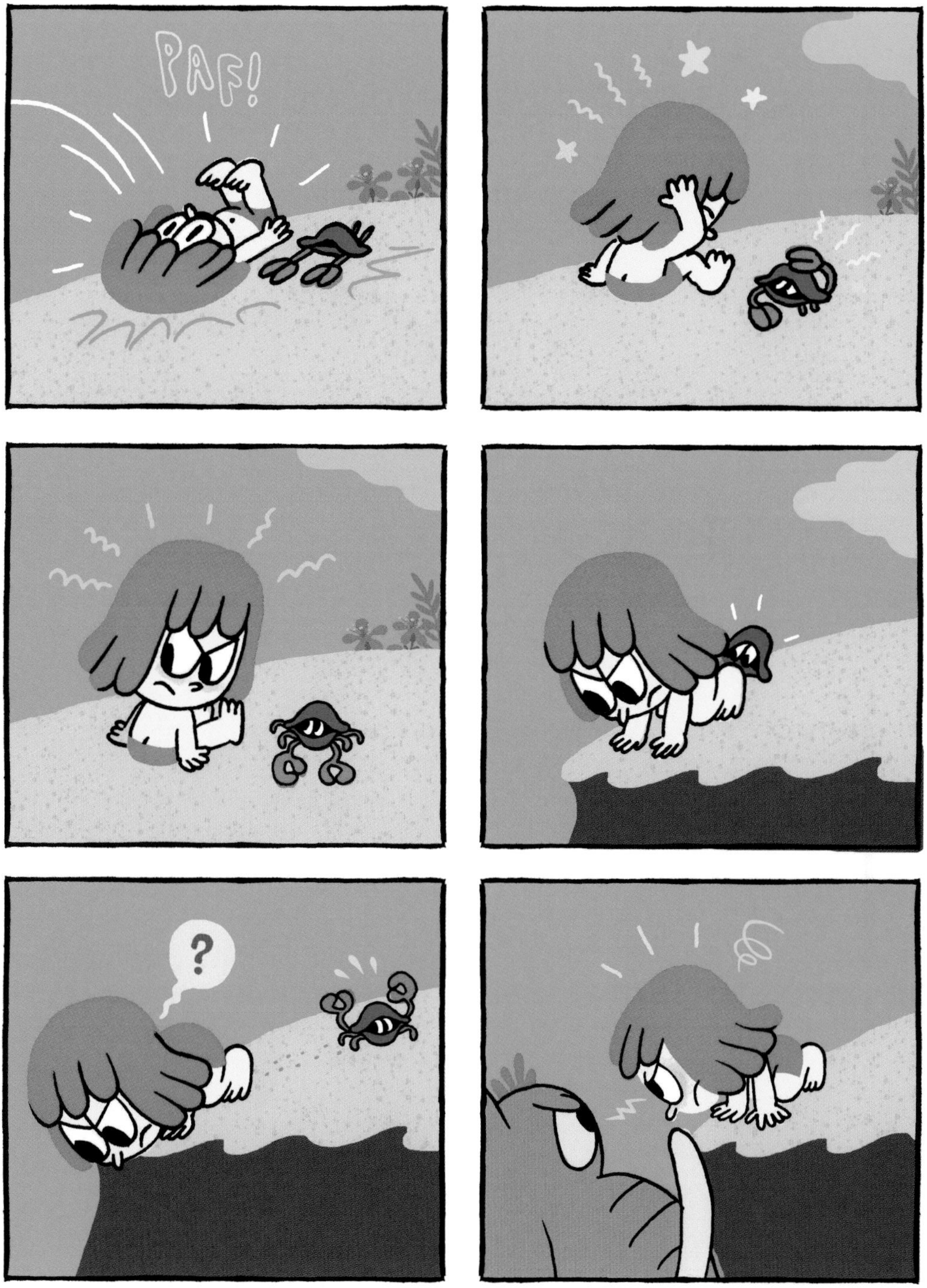
PAF!
?

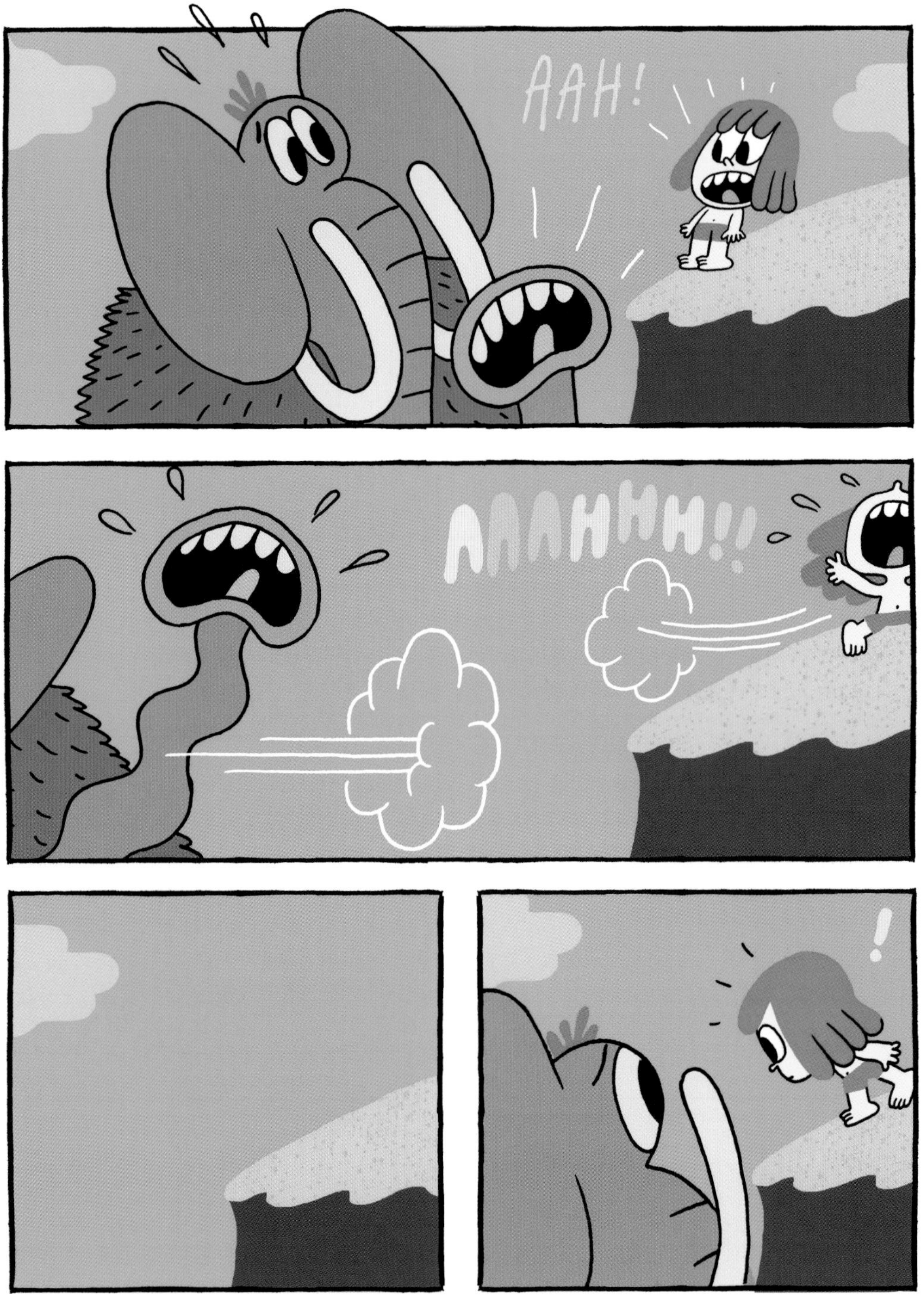
AAH!
AAAHHHH!!!
!

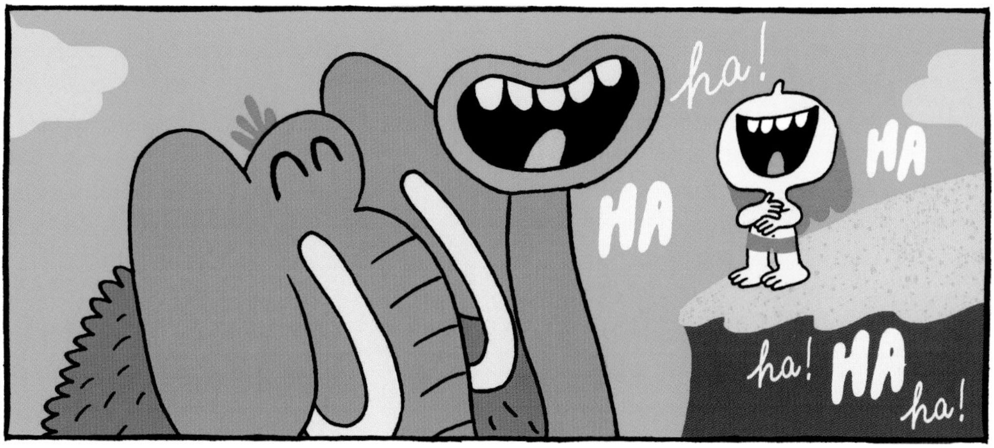
ha!
HA
HA
ha! HA ha!

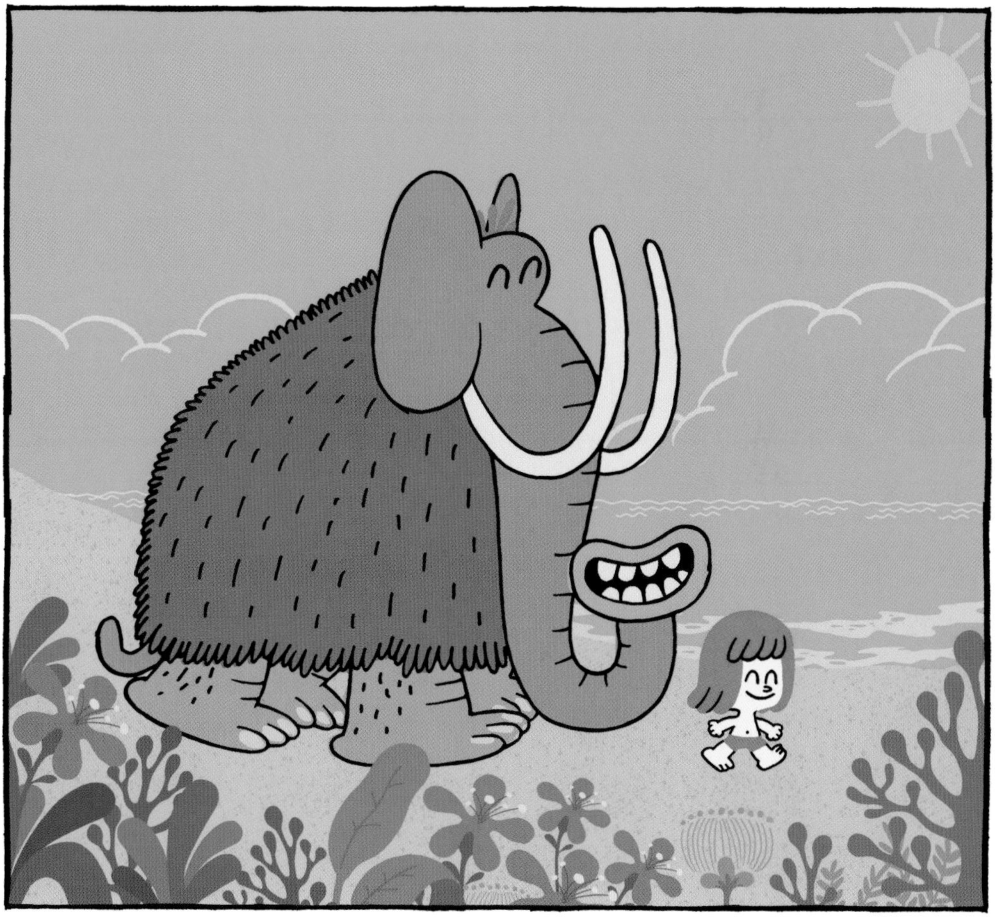

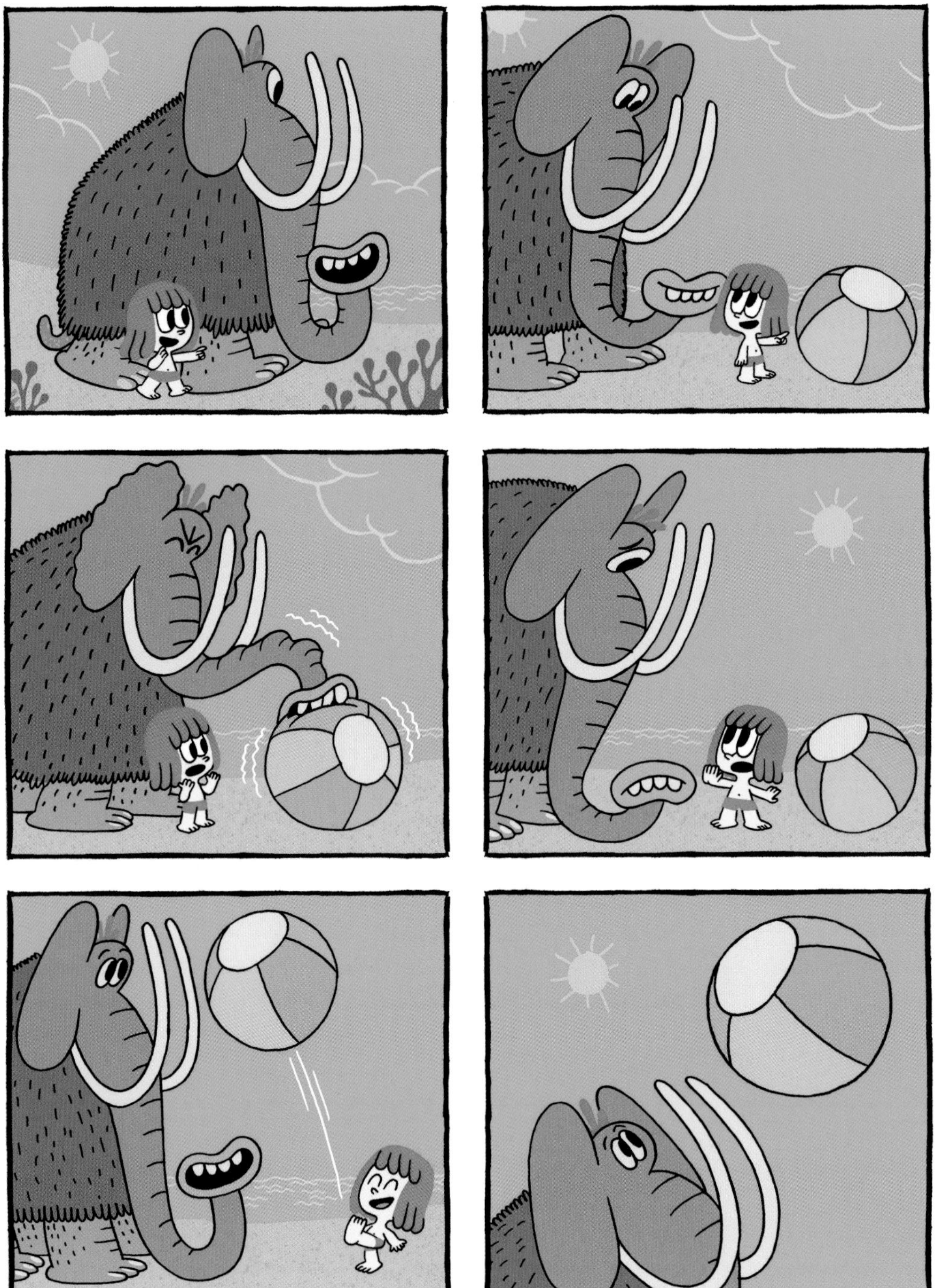

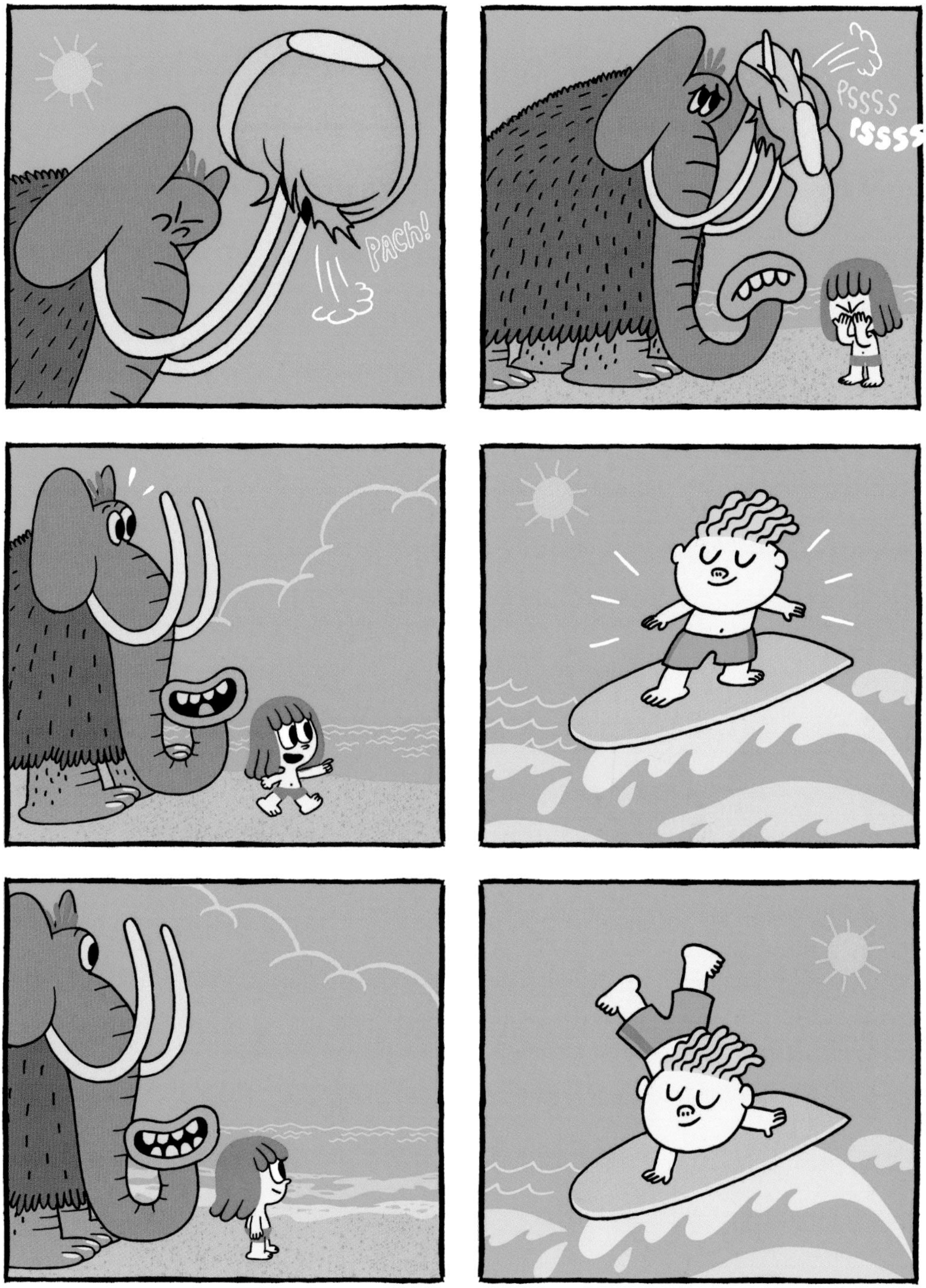
PACH!
PSSSS
ISSS

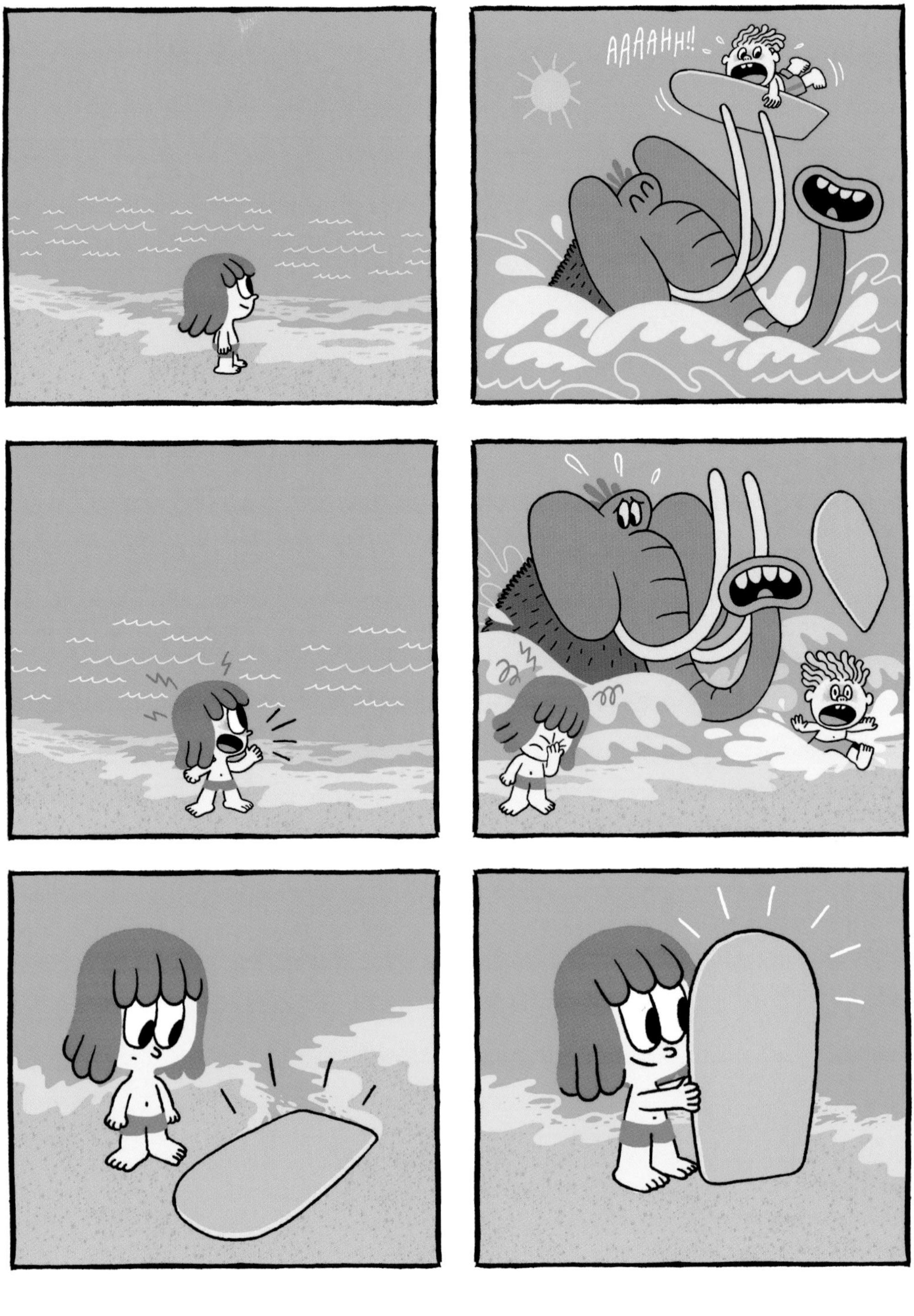
AAAAHH!!

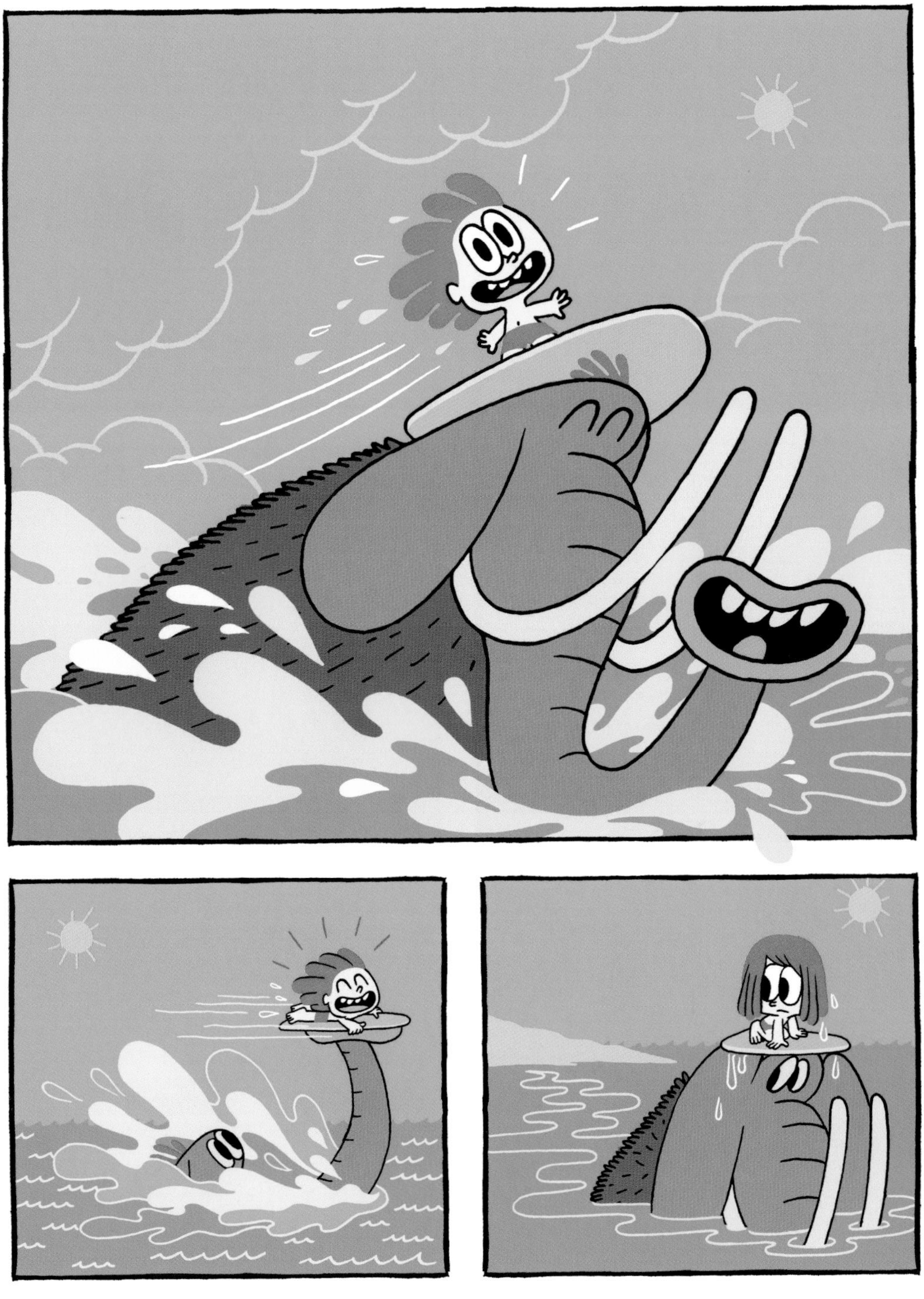

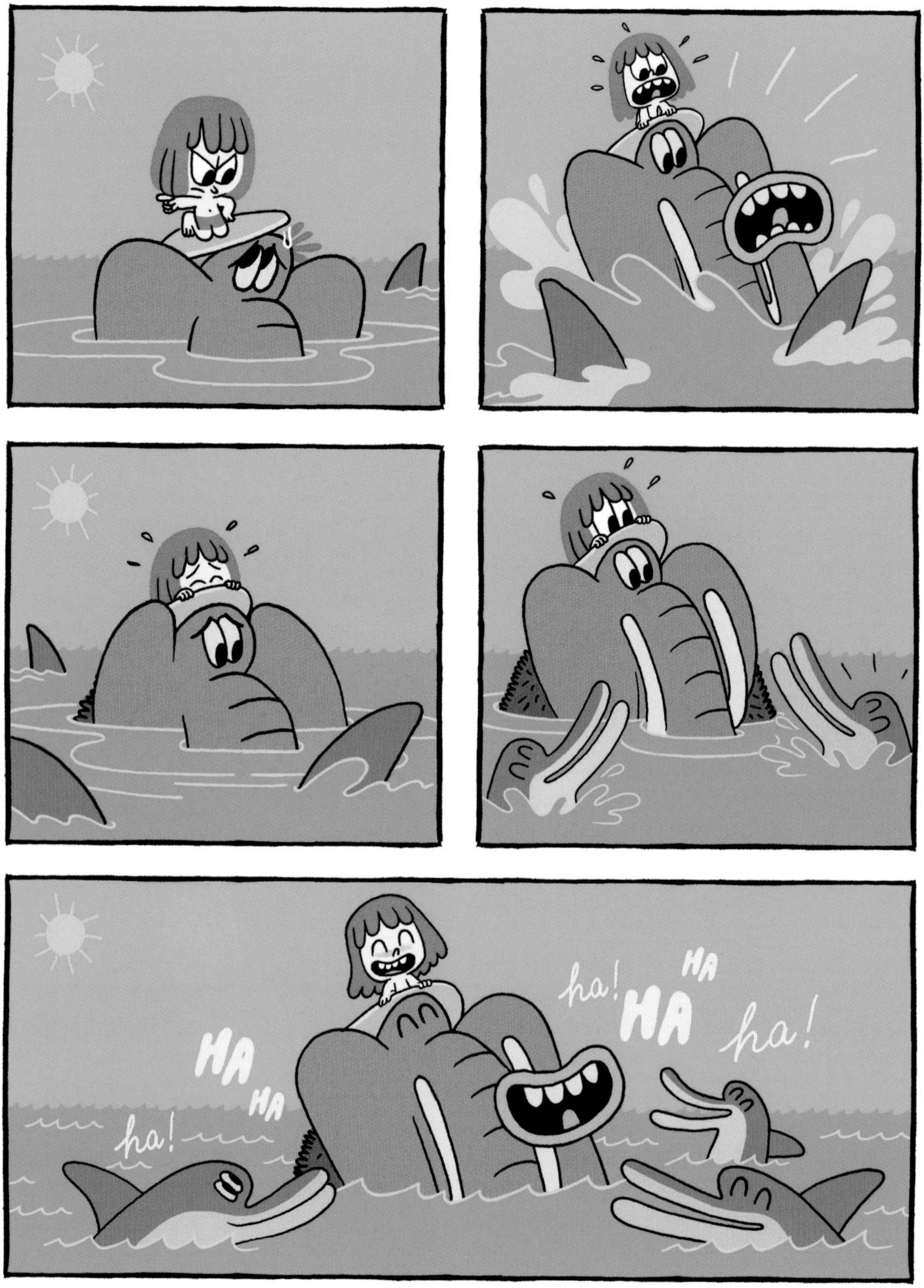
ha!
HA
HA
ha!
HA
HA
ha!

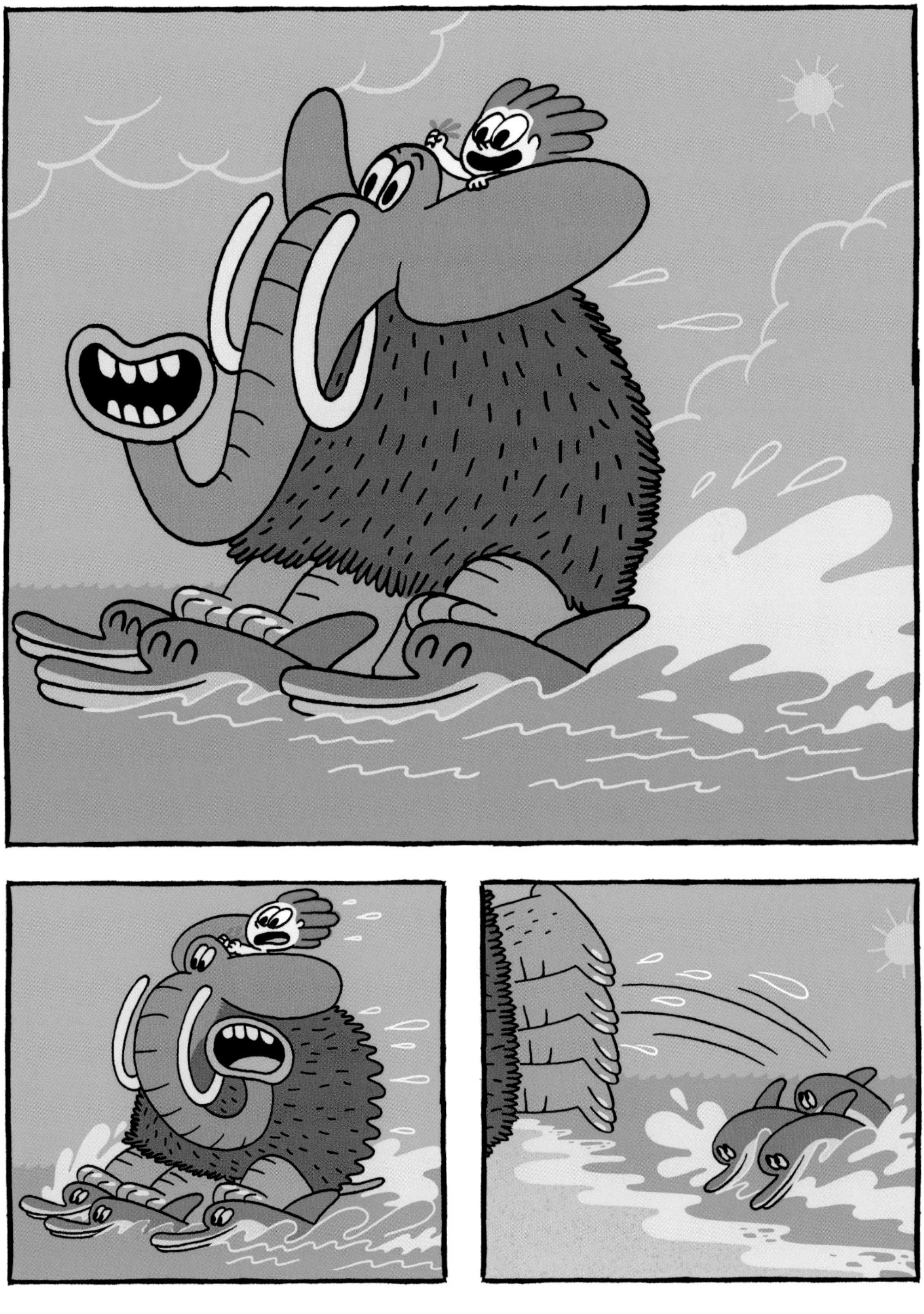

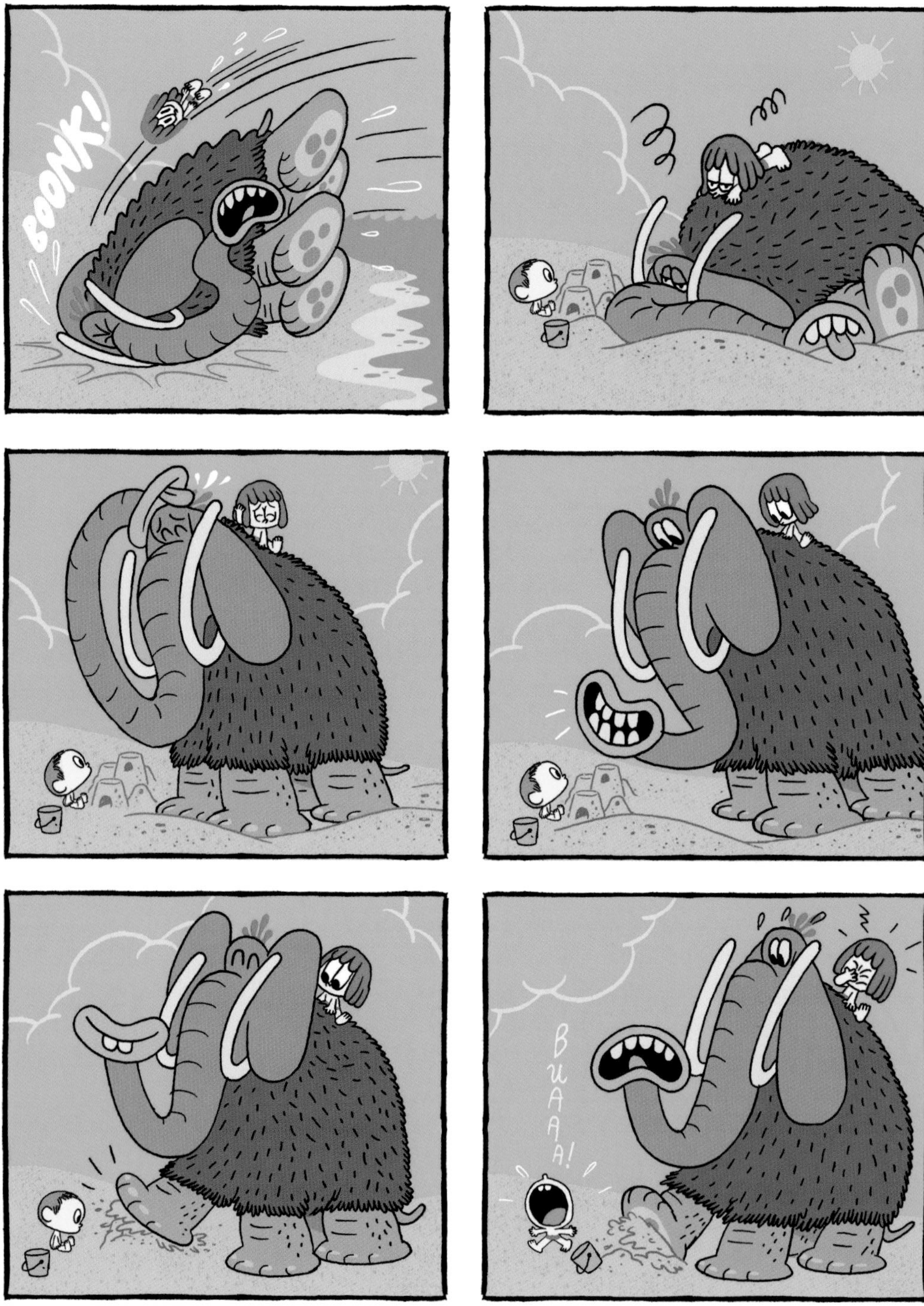
BOONK!
BWAAAA!

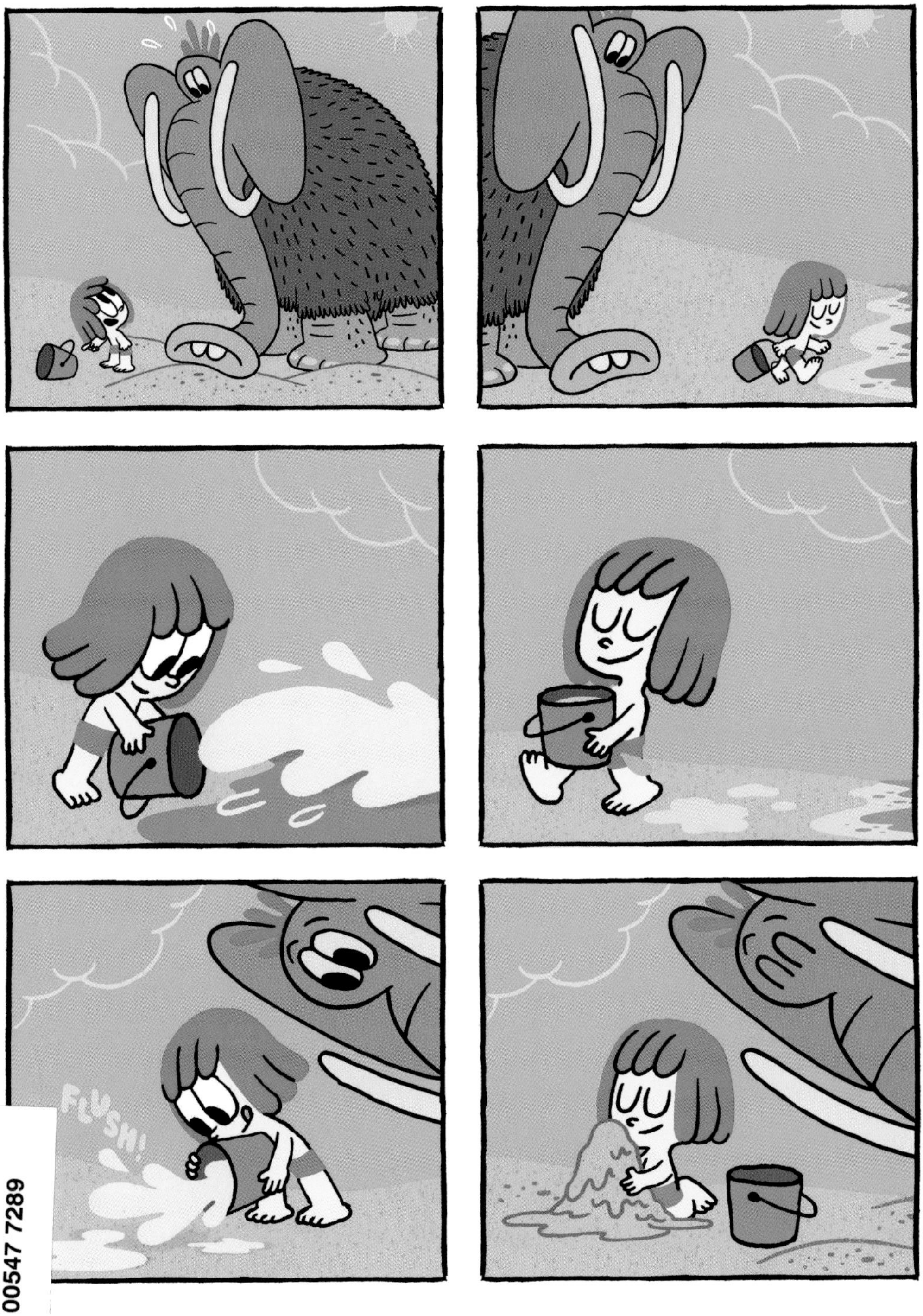
FLUSH!

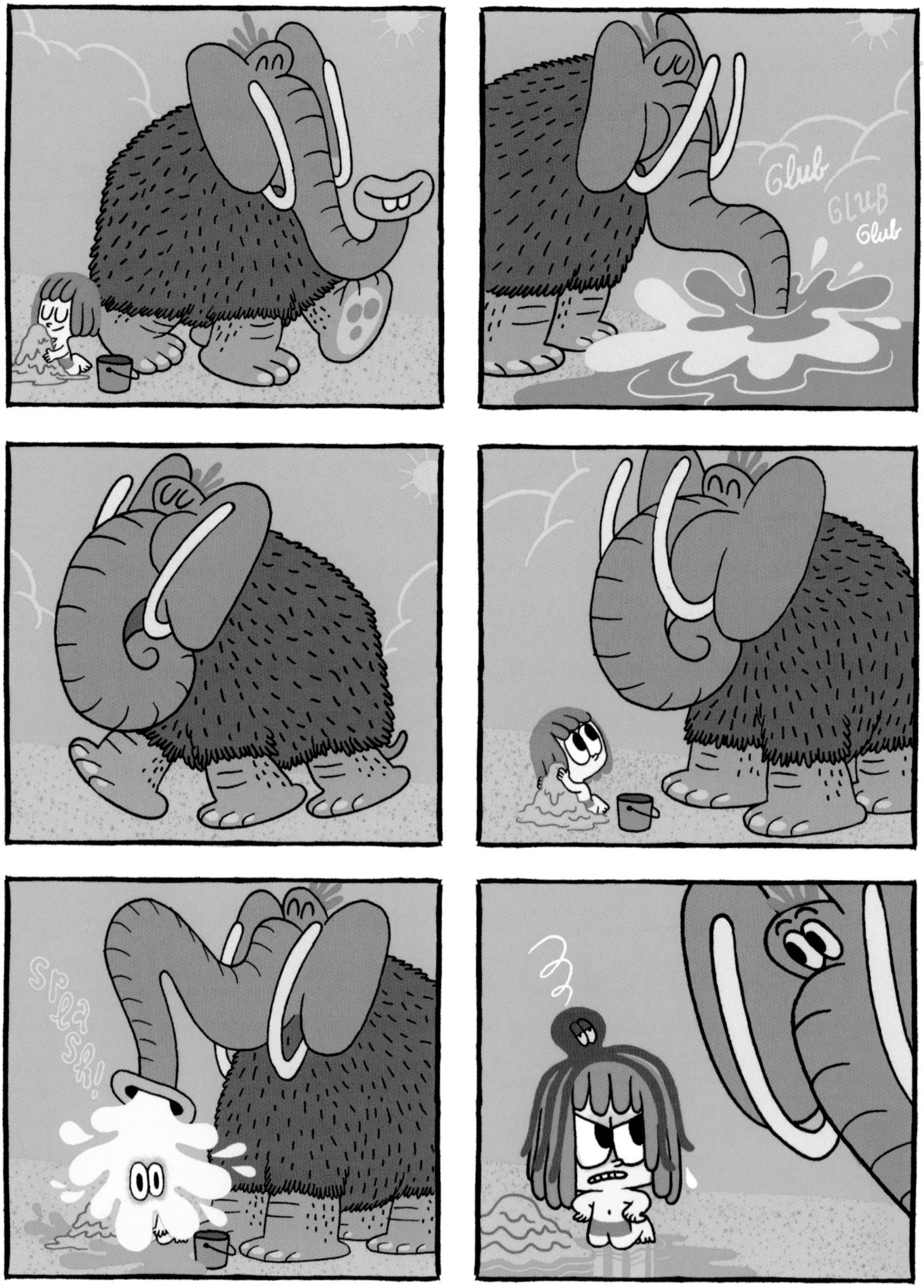
Glub
GLUB
Glub
Splash!

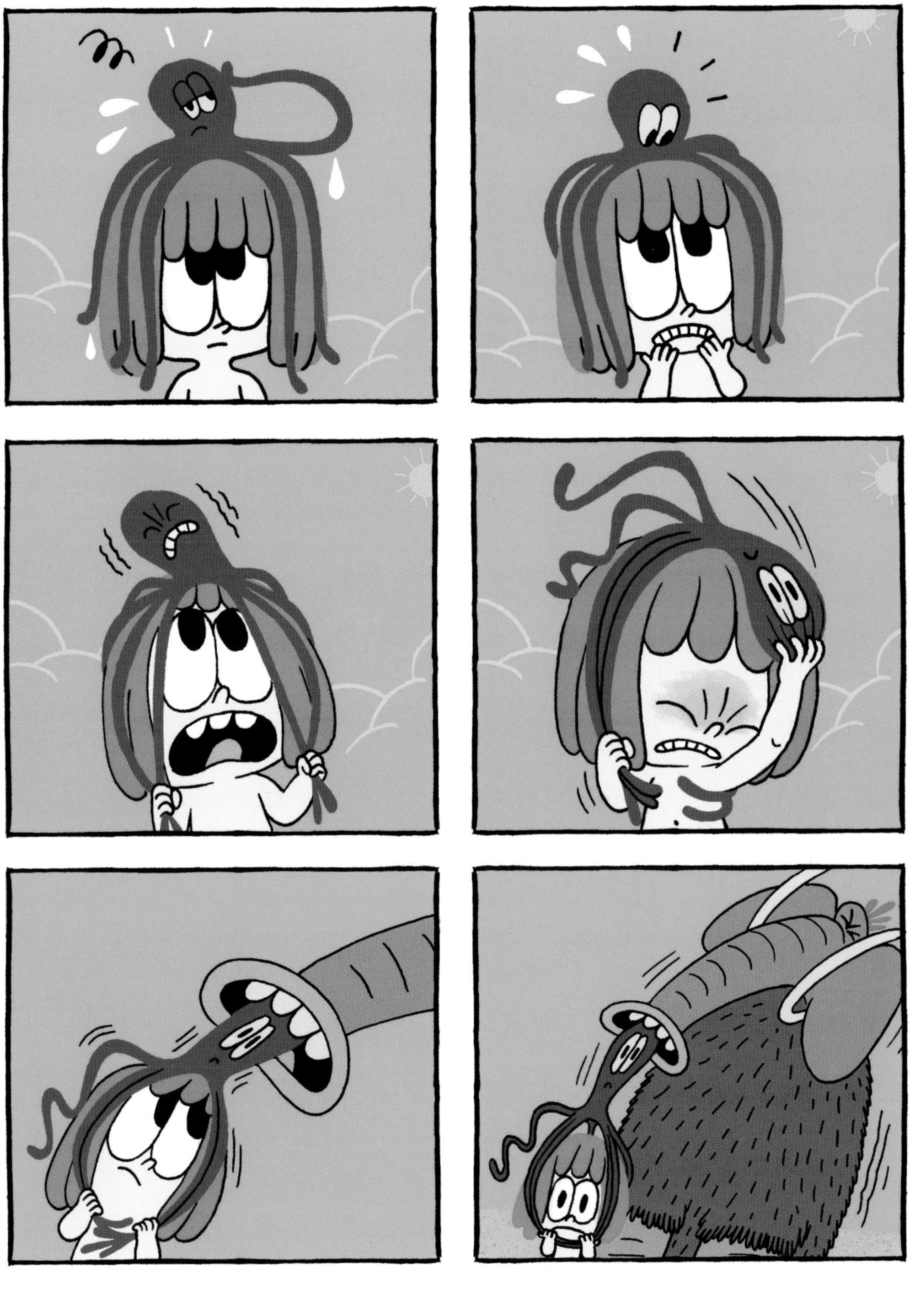

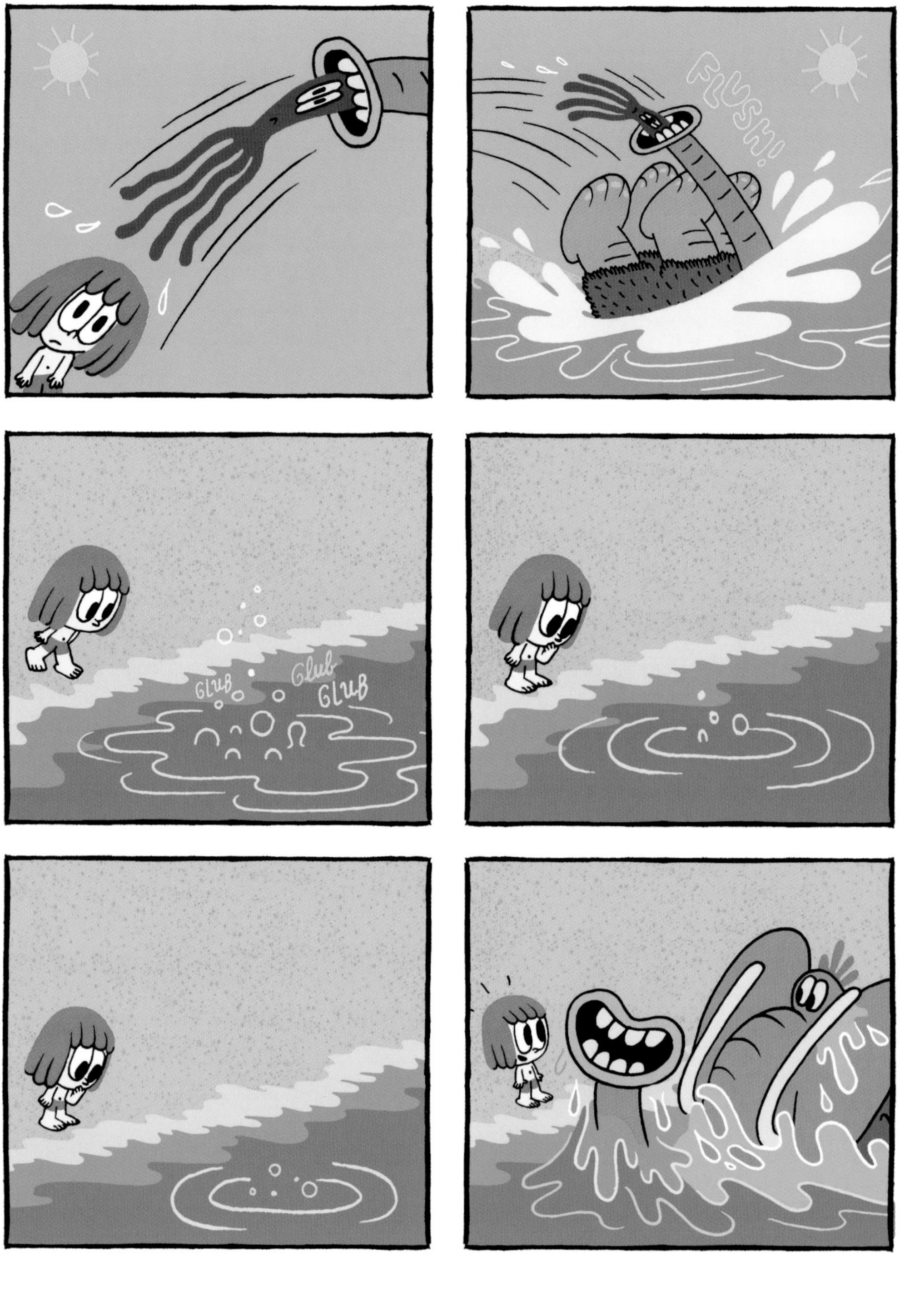
FLUSH!
GLUB
Glub
GLUB

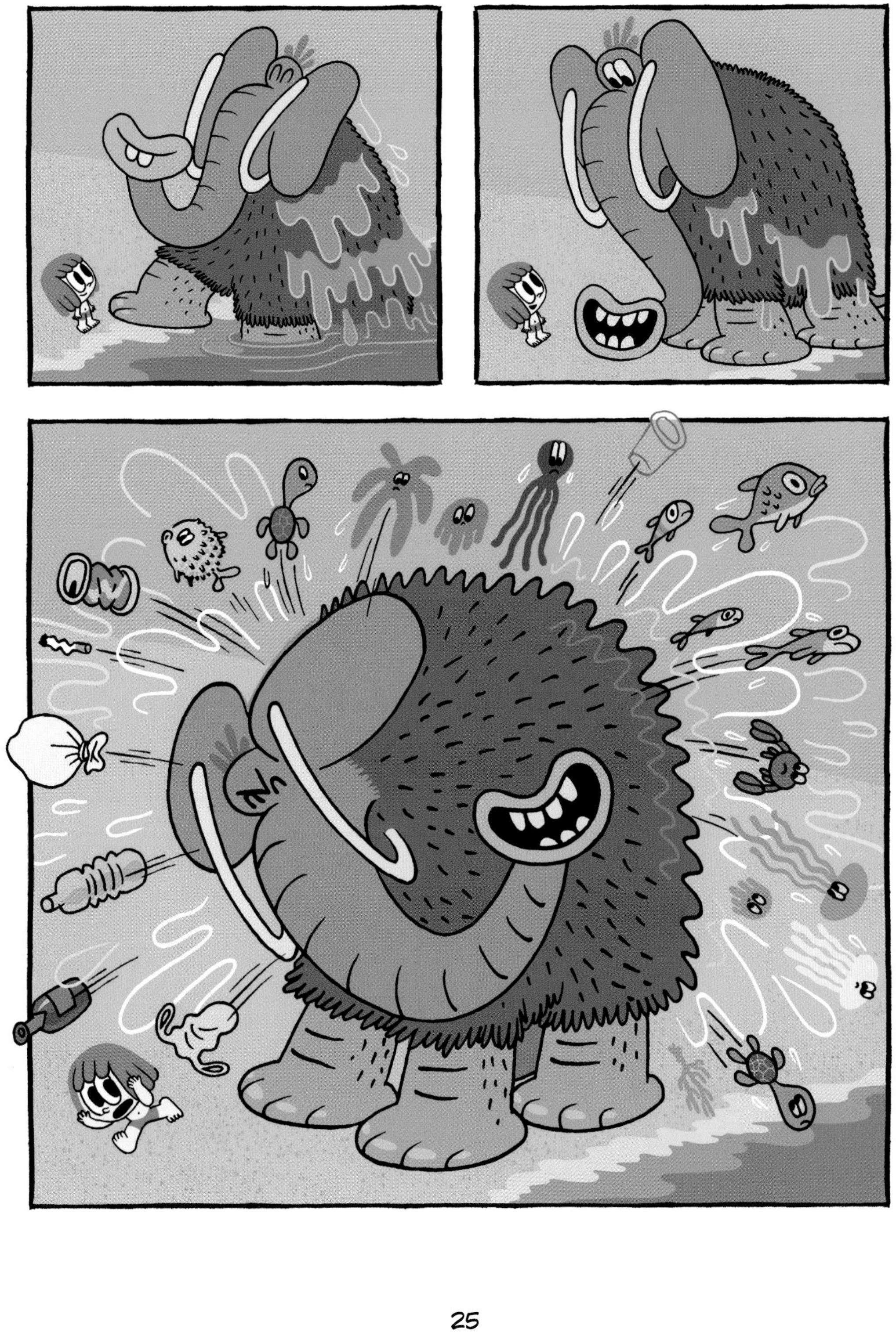

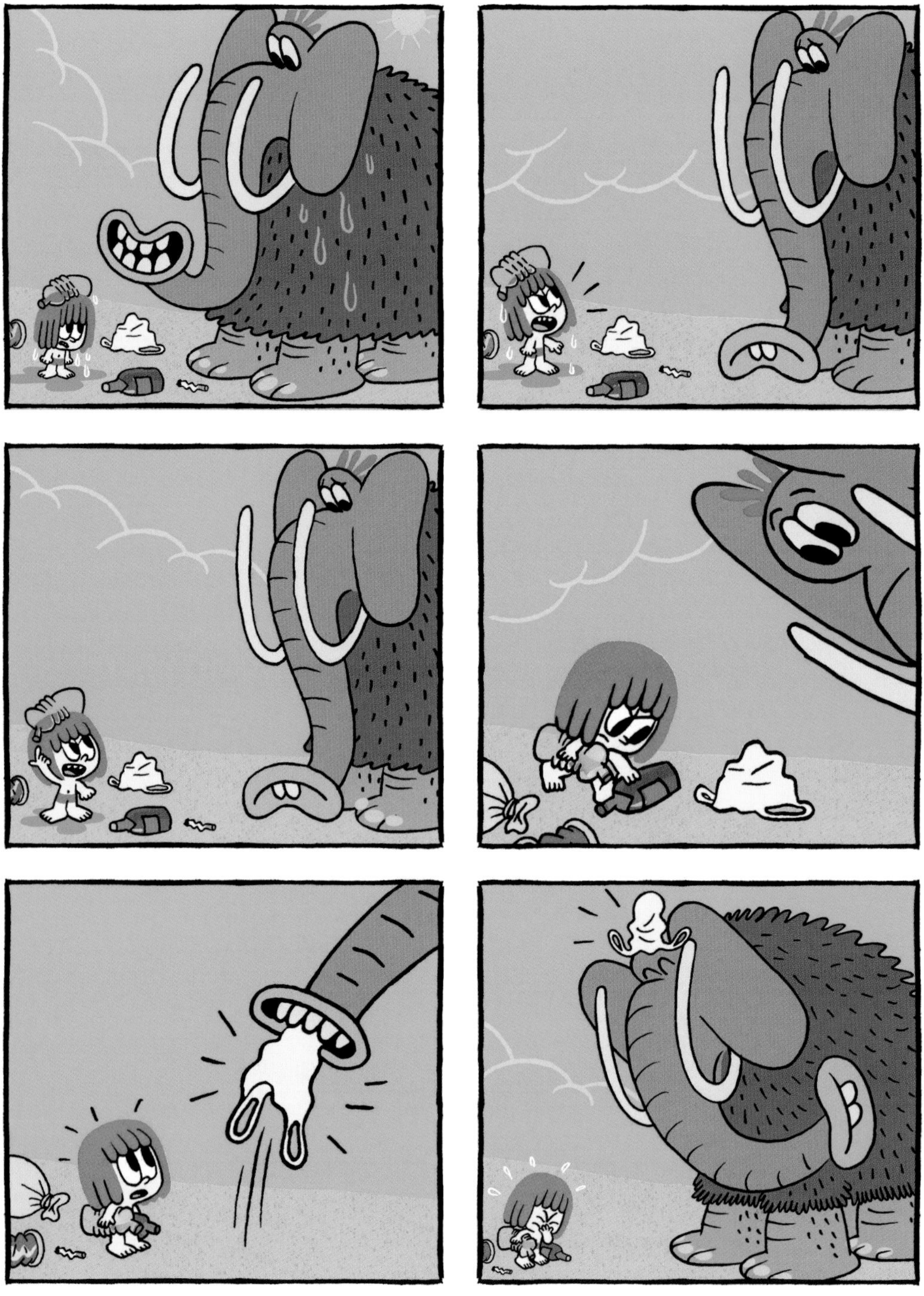

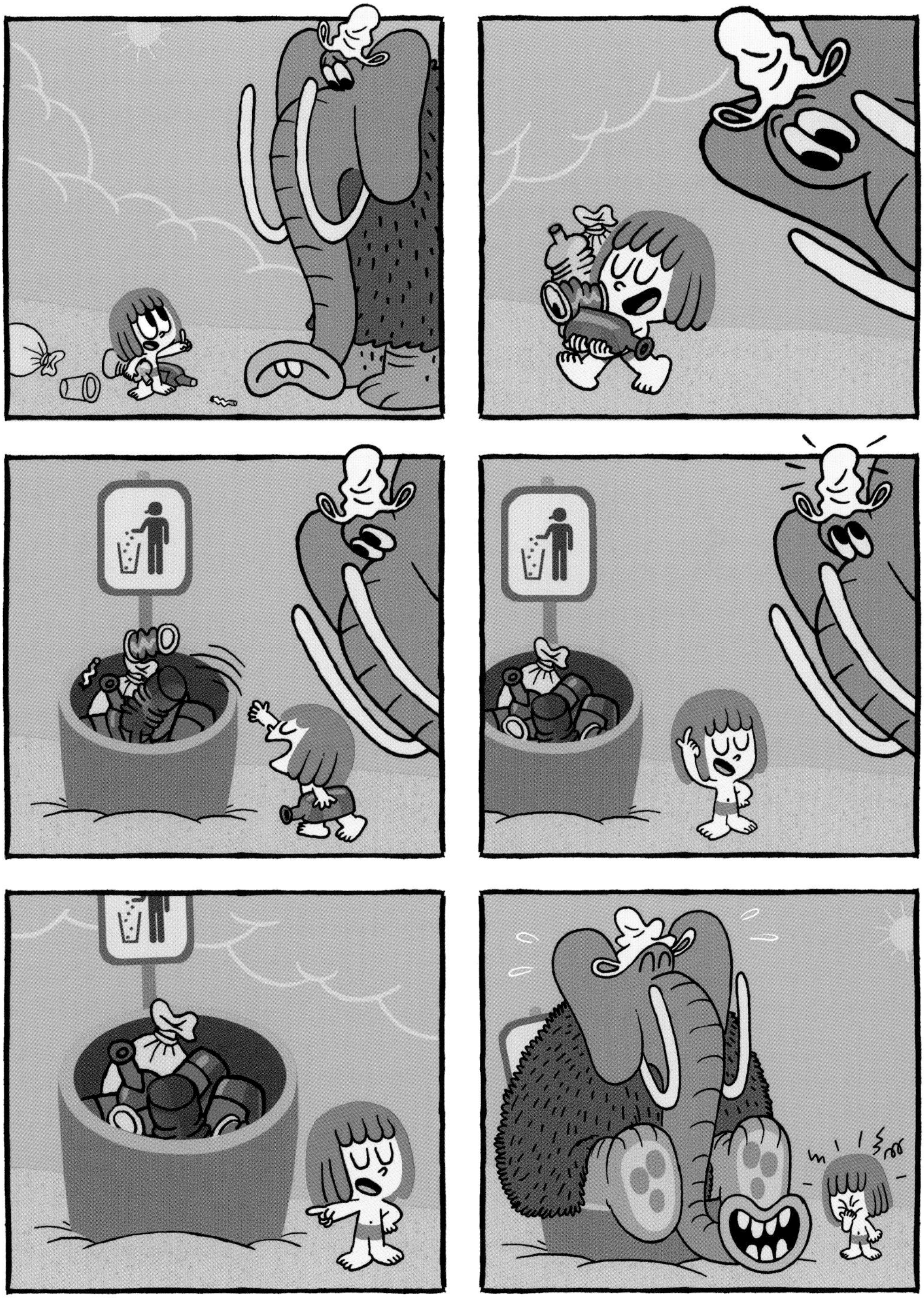

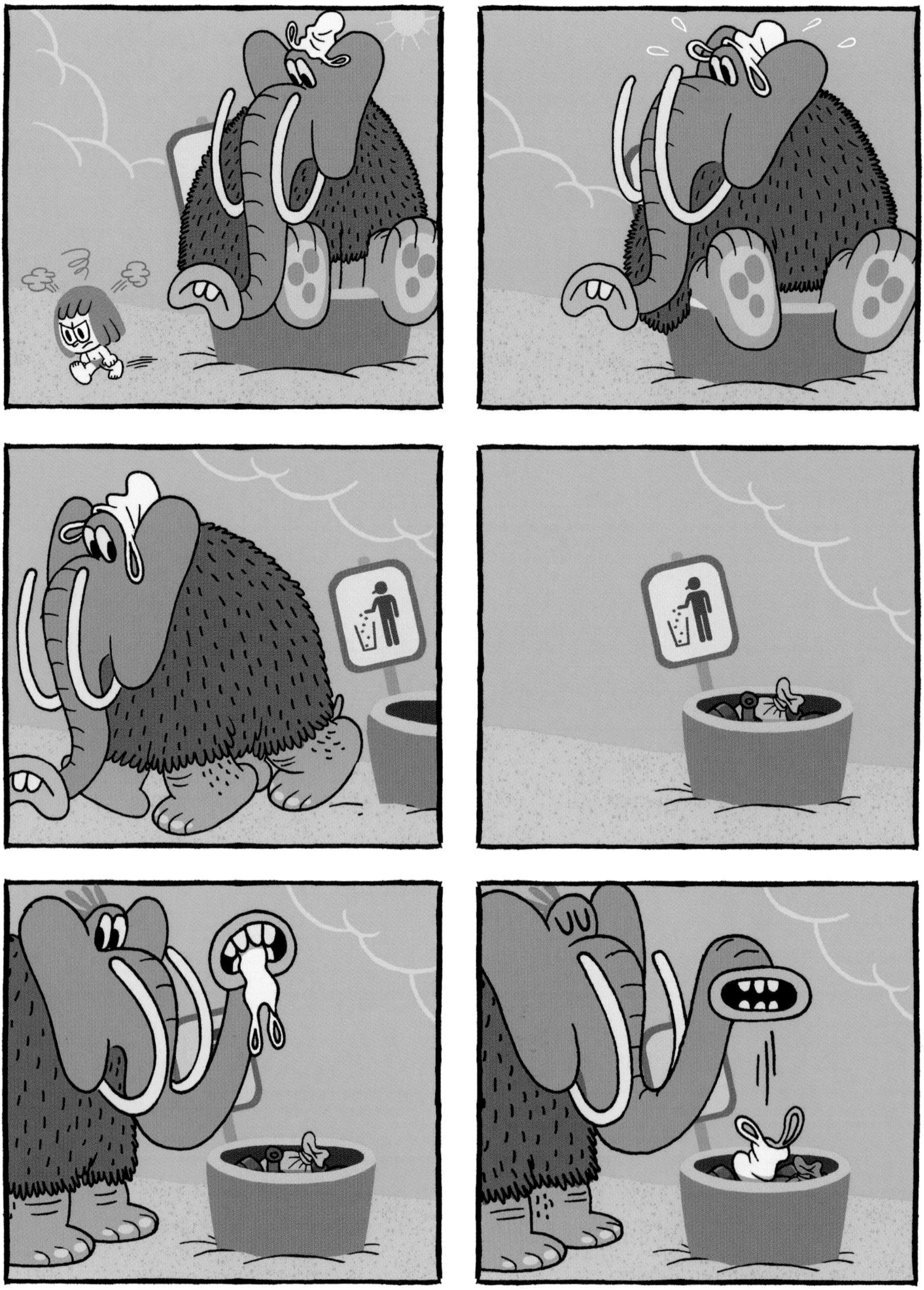

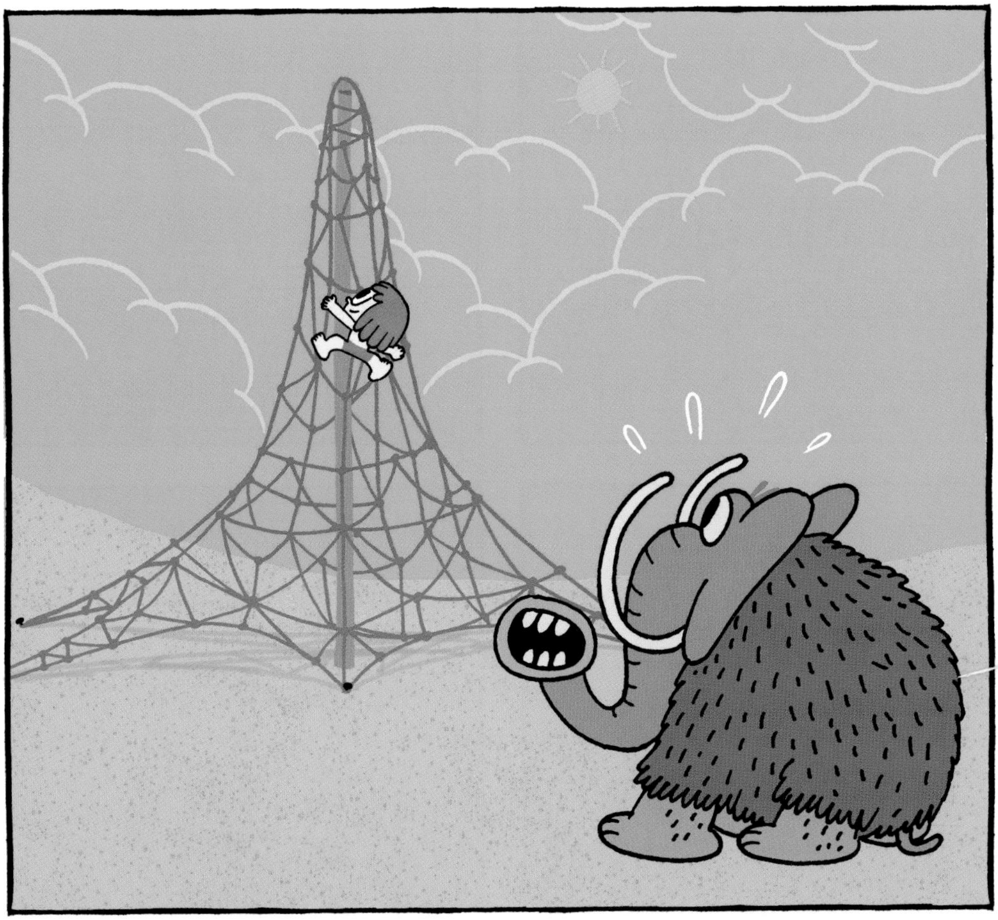

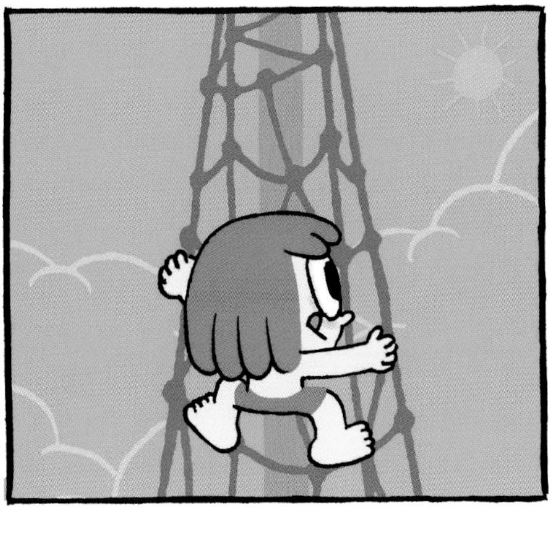

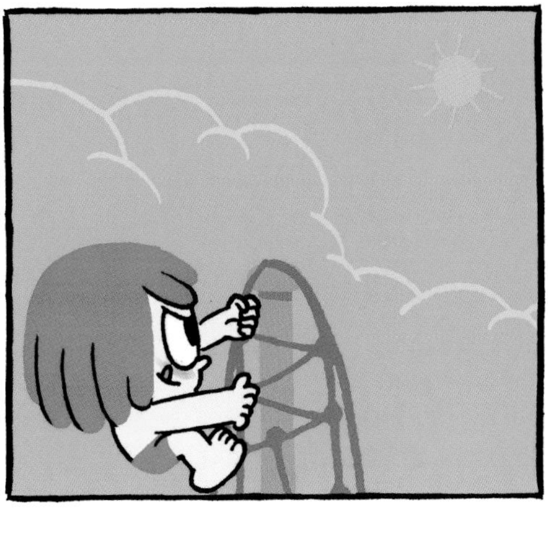

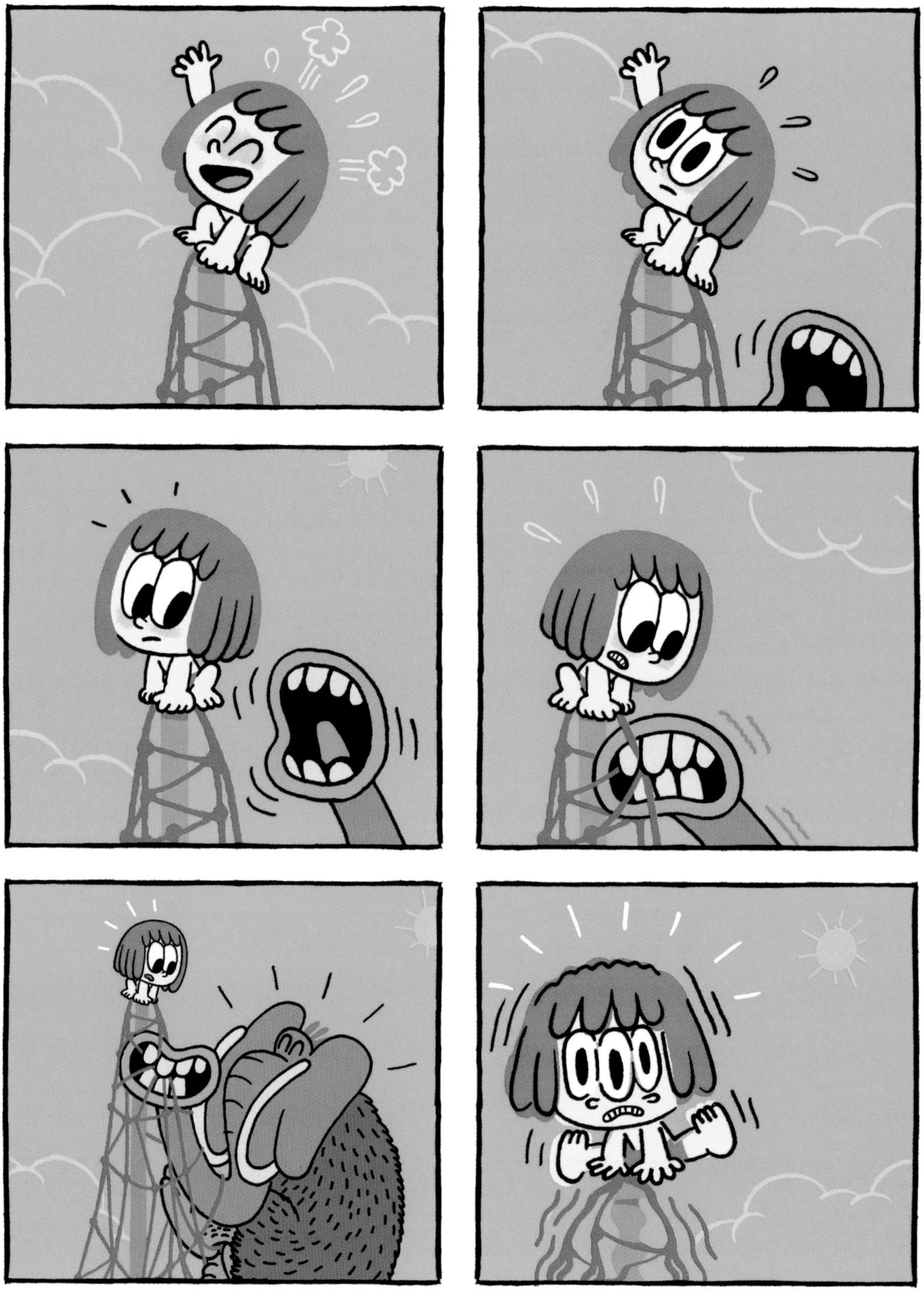

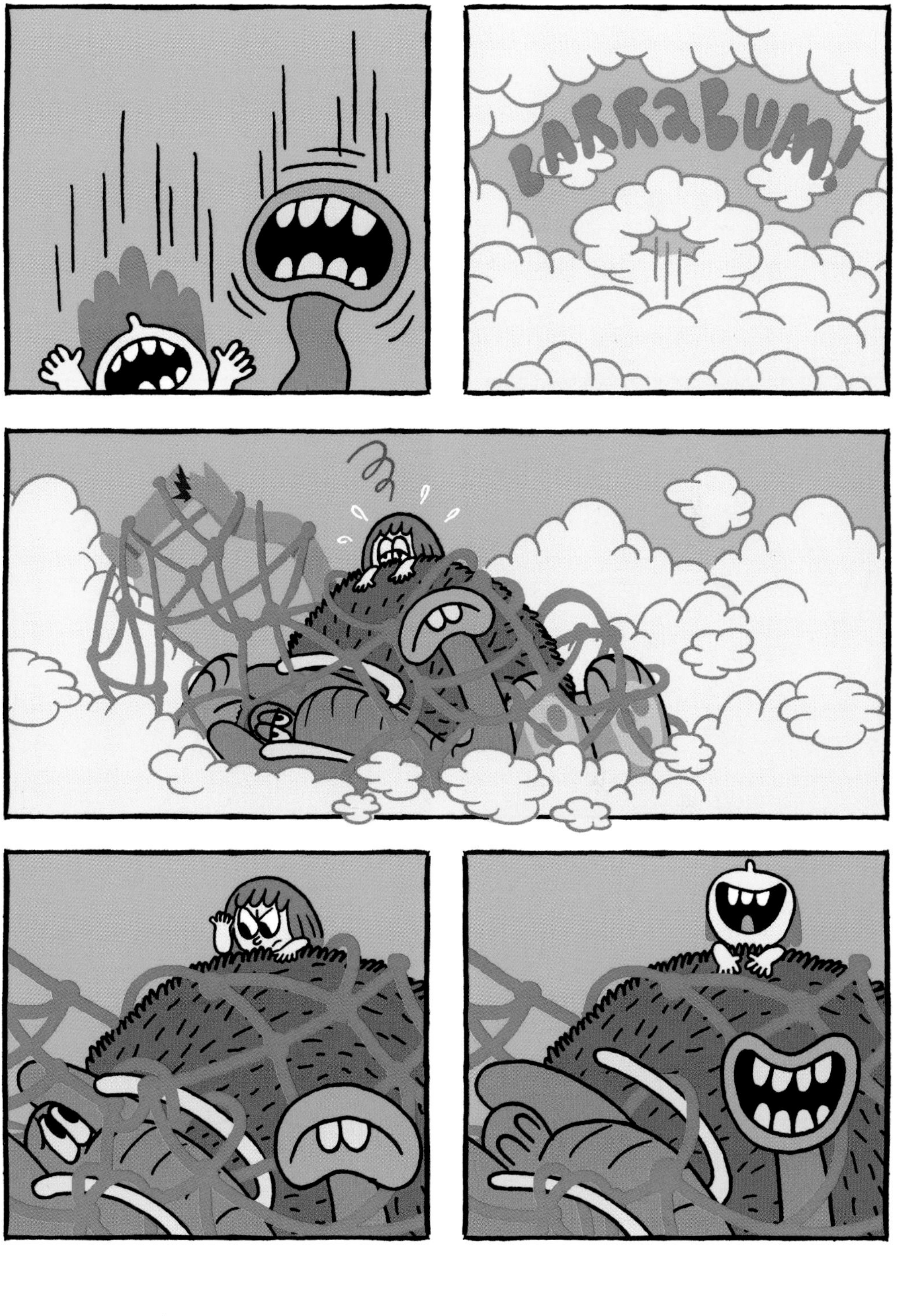
BARRABUM!

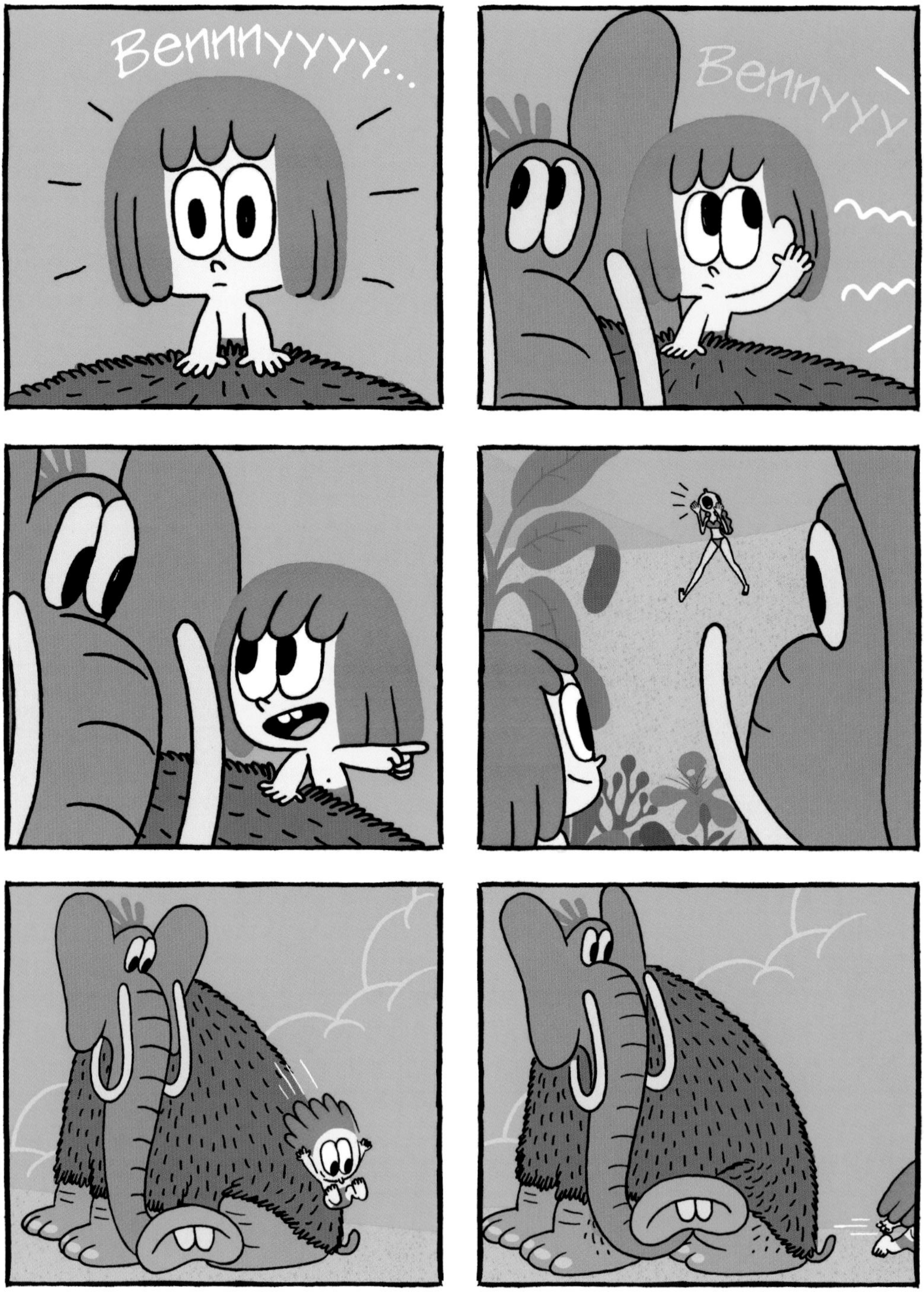
Bennnyyyy...
Bennyyy

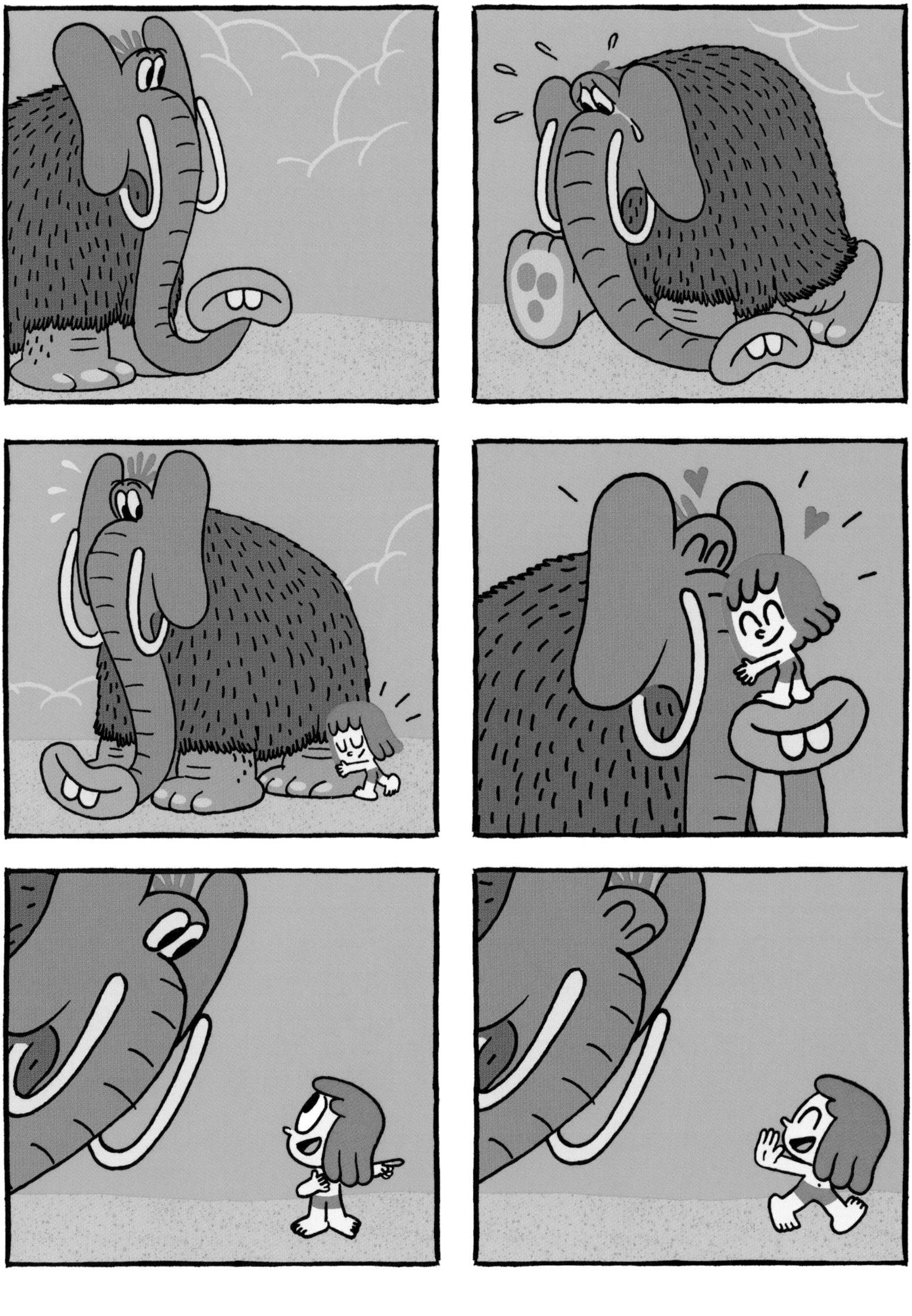

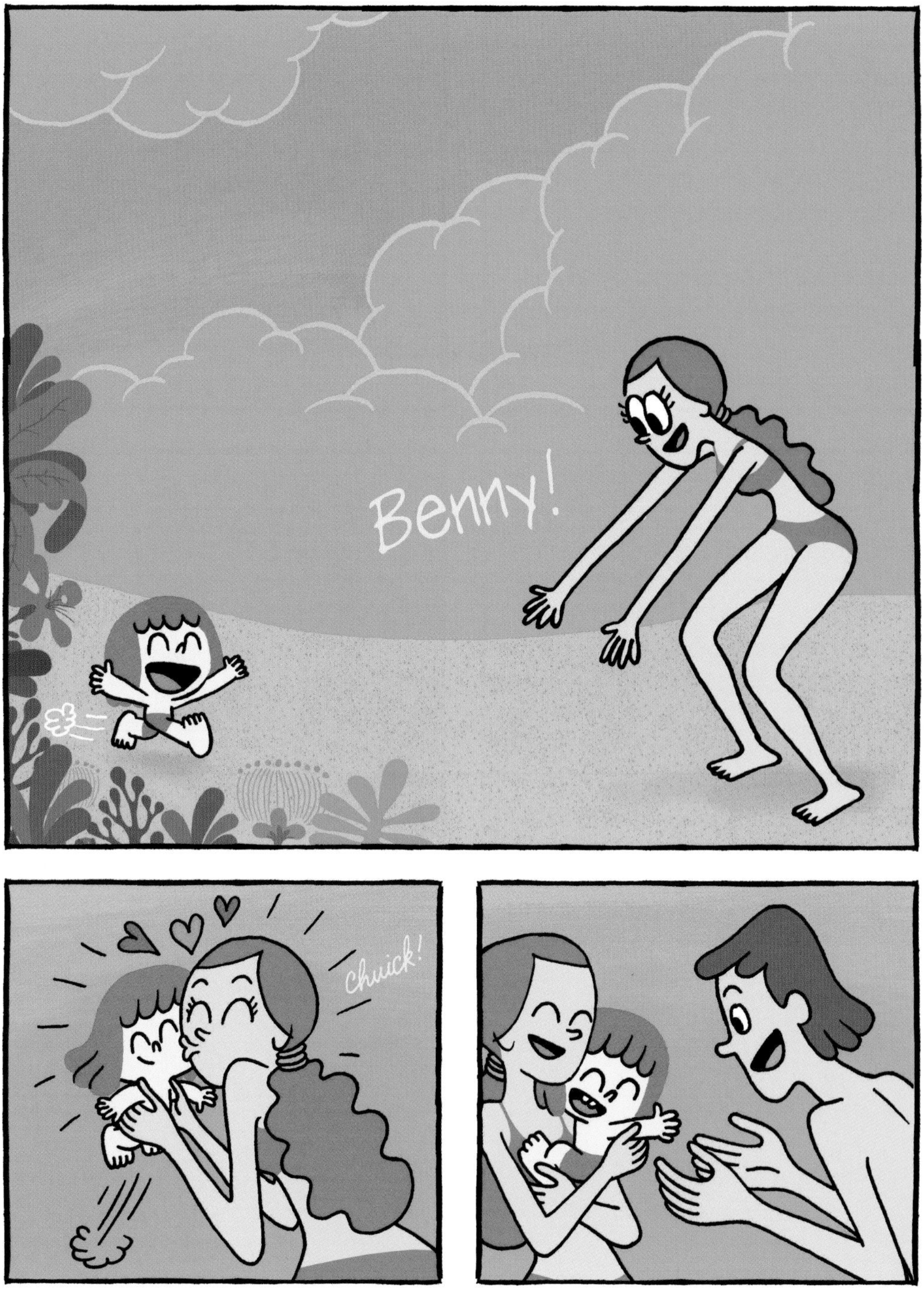
Benny!
Chuick!

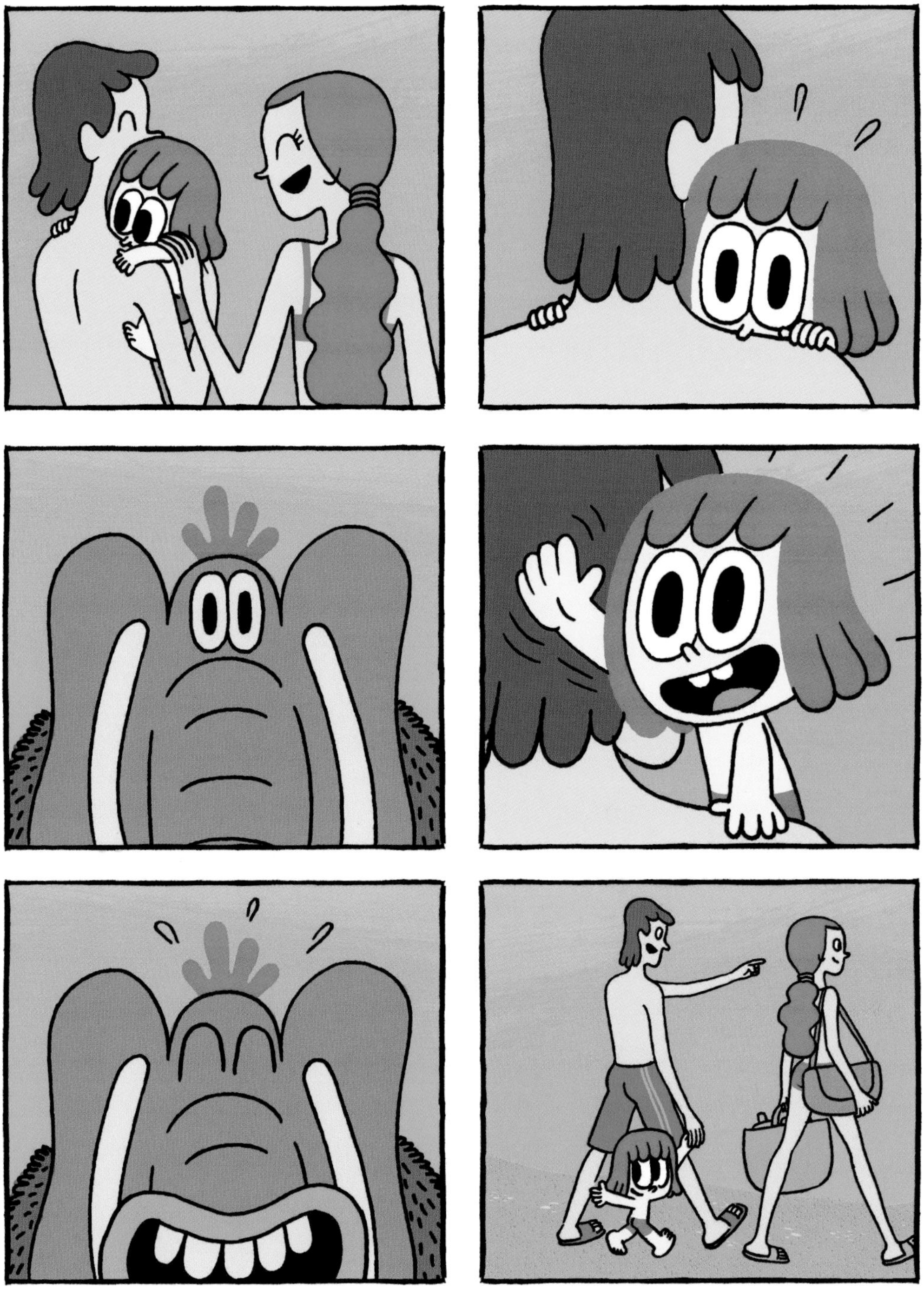

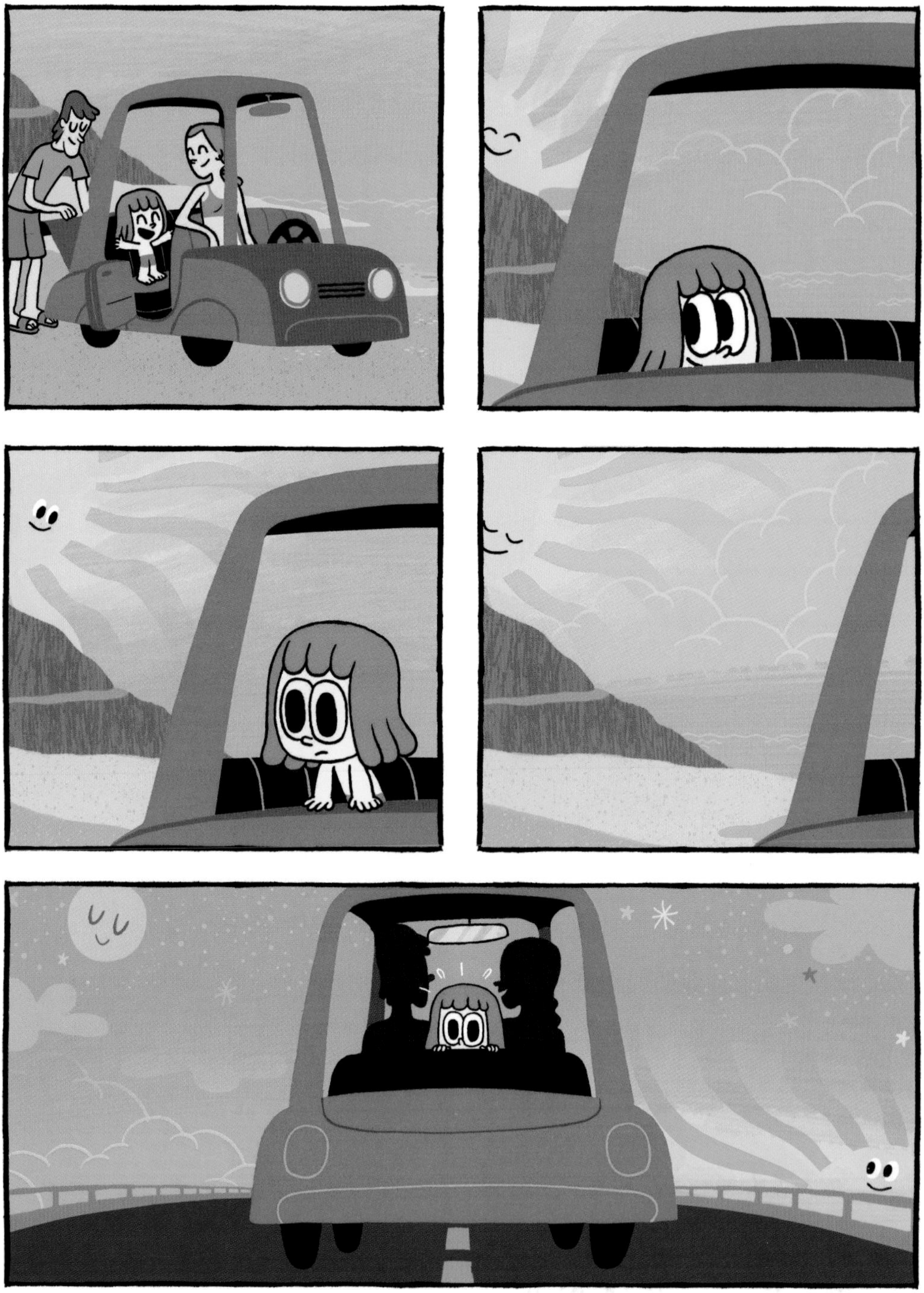

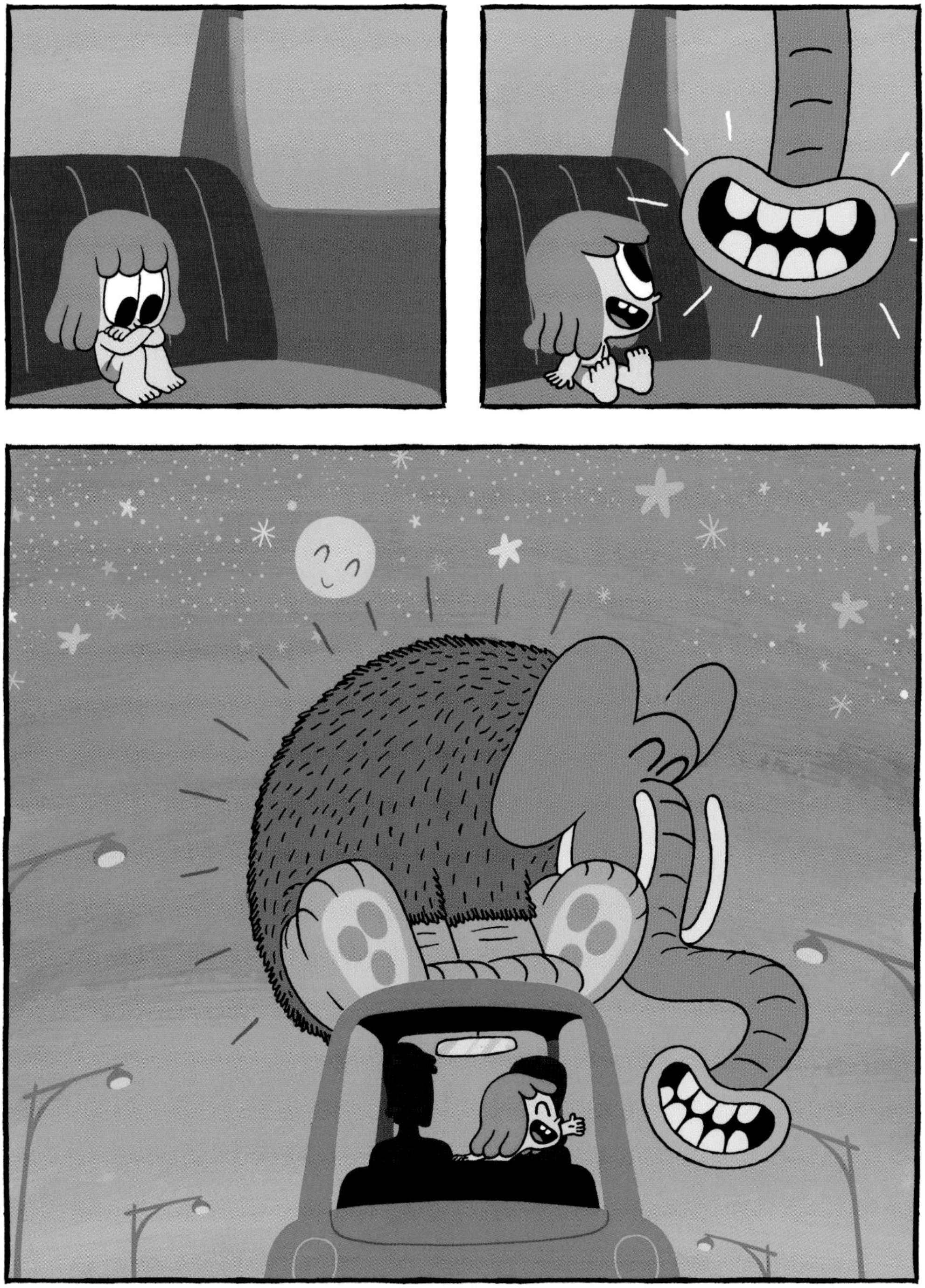

VISUAL QUESTIONS

Benny's mood changes between these panels. How does it change, and what changes it?

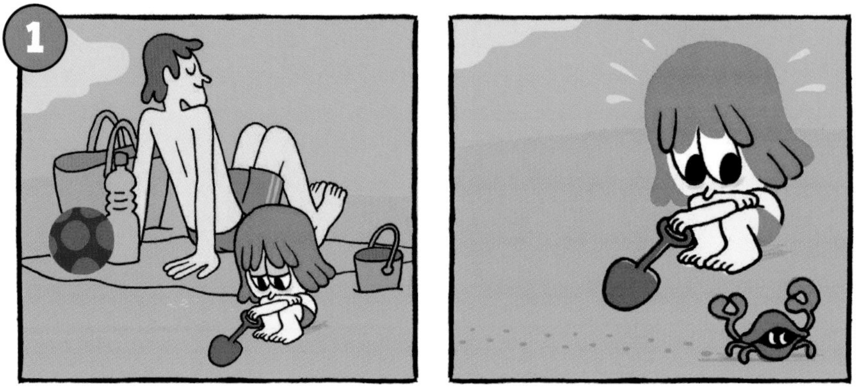
1

What is Benny trying to teach the woolly mammoth in the first three panels? What does the last panel tell you about the mammoth and Benny?

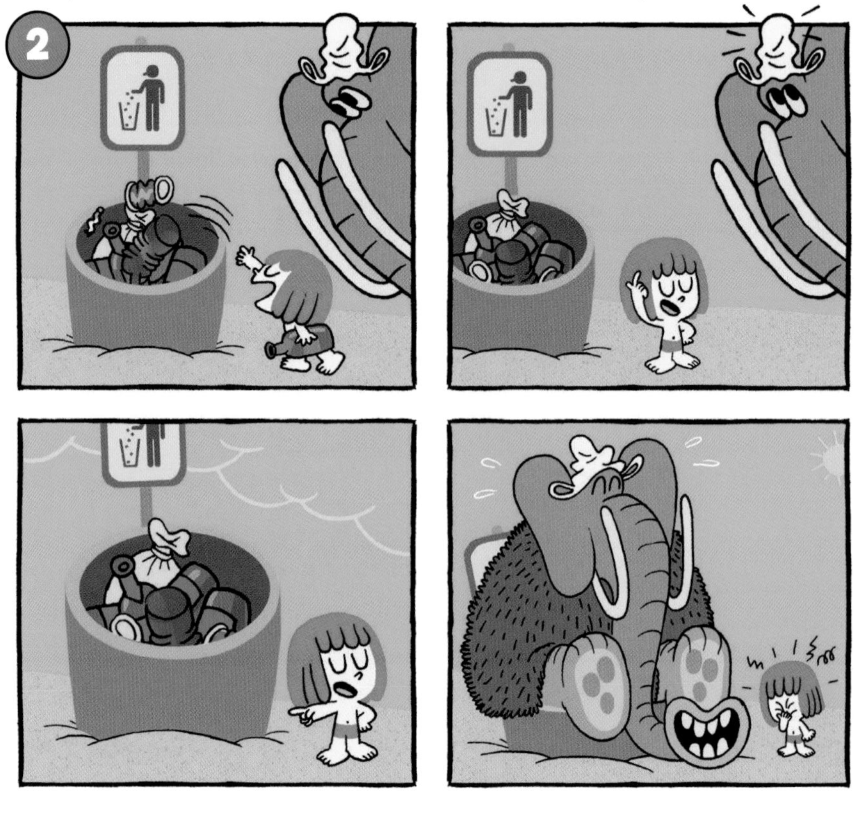
2

How does the octopus feel about being on Benny's head? How does Benny feel? Which character do you feel sorrier for?

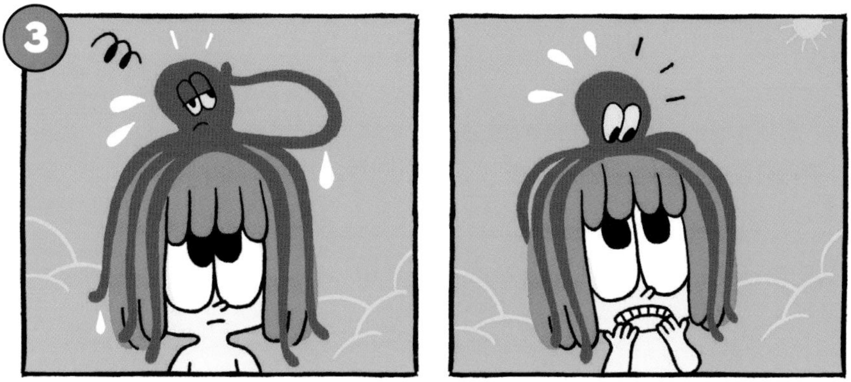
3

What does this panel tell you about the ocean near Benny's beach?

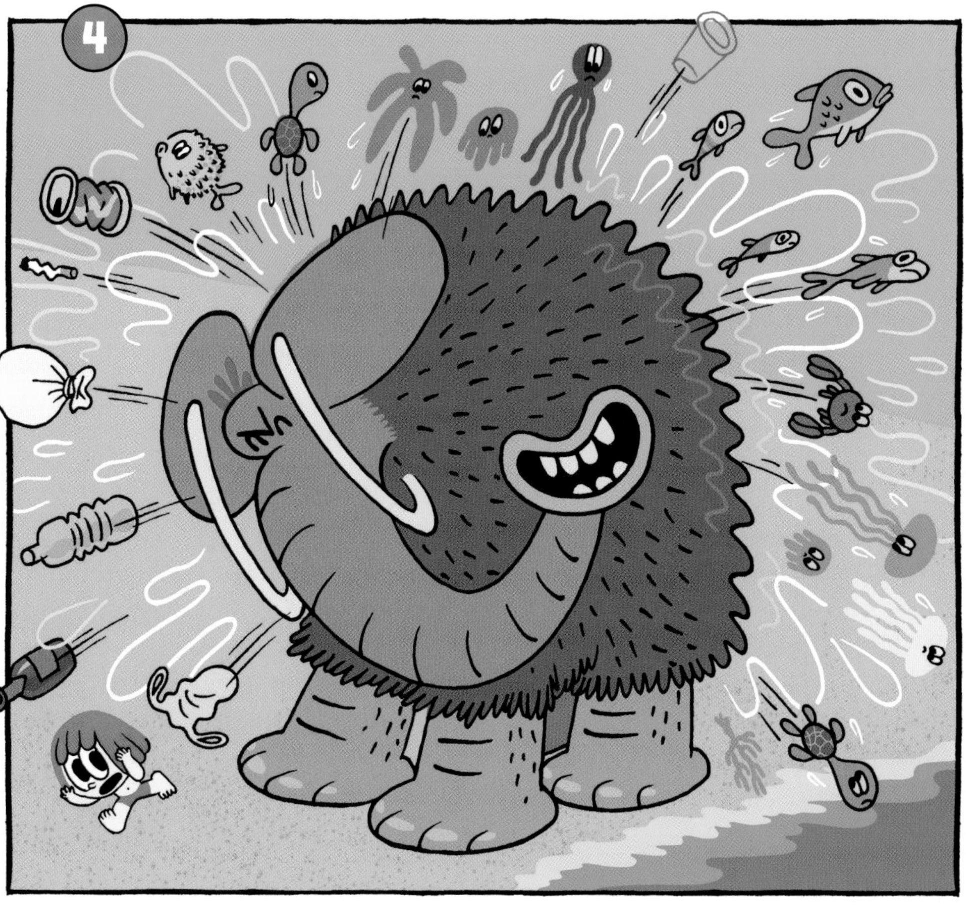
4

READ THEM ALL!

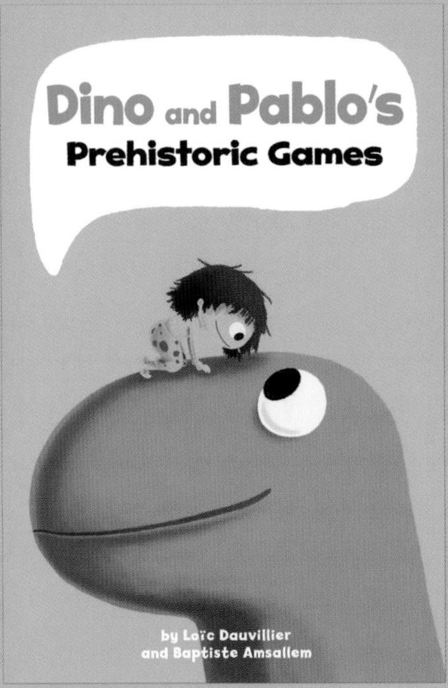
Dino and Pablo's
Prehistoric Games
by Loïc Dauvillier
and Baptiste Amsallem

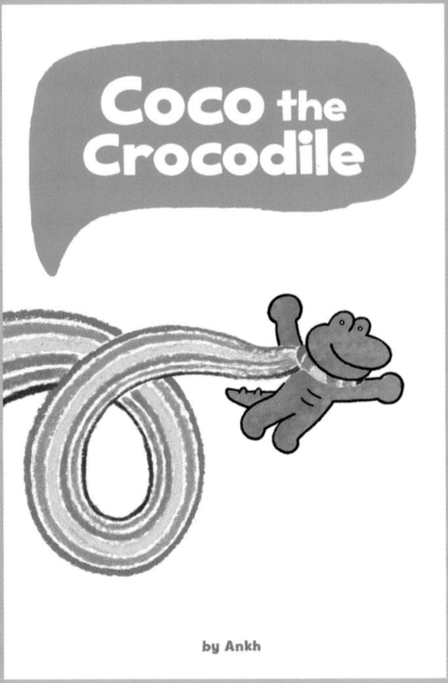
Coco the
Crocodile
by Ankh

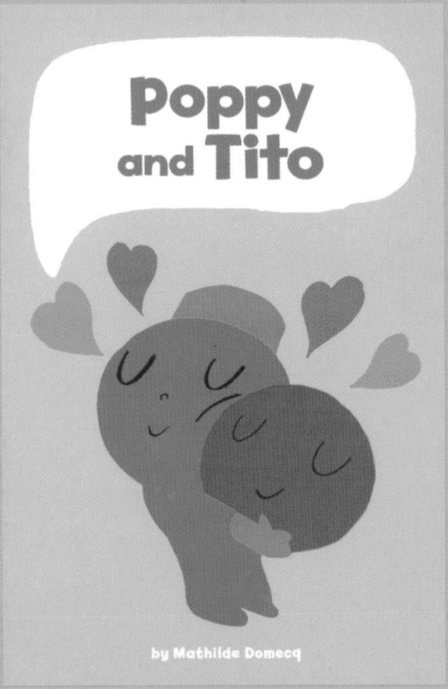
Poppy
and Tito
by Mathilde Domecq

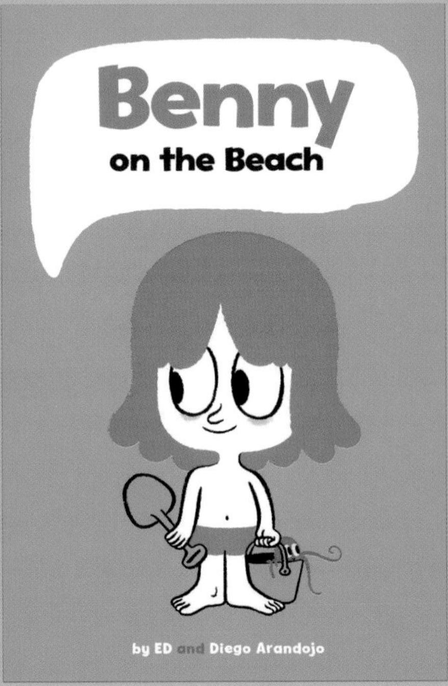
Benny
on the Beach
by ED and Diego Arandojo